The Gatekeeper

A Dark Bratva Romance

Chicago Bratva

Renee Rose

Copyright © January 2023 The Gatekeeper by Renee Rose and Renee Rose Romance

All rights reserved. This copy is intended for the original purchaser of this book ONLY. No part of this book may be reproduced, scanned, or distributed in any printed or electronic form without prior written permission from the authors. Please do not participate in or encourage piracy of copyrighted materials in violation of the authors' rights. Purchase only authorized editions.

Published in the United States of America

Wilrose Dream Ventures LLC

Cover by: Pop Kitty Designs

This book is a work of fiction. While reference might be made to actual historical events or existing locations, the names, characters, places and incidents are either the product of the authors' imaginations or are used fictitiously, and any resemblance to actual persons, living or dead, business establishments, events, or locales is entirely coincidental.

This book contains descriptions of many BDSM and sexual practices, but this is a work of fiction and, as such, should not be used in any way as a guide. The author and publisher will not be responsible for any loss, harm, injury, or death resulting from use of the information contained within. In other words, don't try this at home, folks!

❦ Created with Vellum

Want FREE Renee Rose books?

Go to http://subscribepage.com/alphastemp to sign up for Renee Rose's newsletter and receive a free copy of *Alpha's Temptation, Theirs to Protect, Owned by the Marine* and more. In addition to the free stories, you will also get bonus epilogues, special pricing, exclusive previews and news of new releases.

Prologue

Kira, 13 years old

A splintering pounding sounds on our front door.

I'm in my nightshirt, brushing my teeth for bed.

My father has been missing for two days. It's not unusual. He has his addictions: alcohol. Gambling. Low-level grifting.

But unlike our mother, he's a decent parent. When he's home, he laughs and jokes with us. He may break every promise he makes, but at least he gives us attention.

Our mom is shut up in her room, as always at this time of night. She's a living ghost. She's emotionally checked out from living with our dad, I guess. She works to pay the rent and put groceries in the refrigerator but, otherwise, barely functions.

I run out to the living room.

"Kira, come here!" My sister, Anya, who is seventeen and more of a mother to me than our own, grabs a butcher knife from the kitchen.

The door bursts open, and our dingy apartment floods with tattooed men.

Bratva. The Russian *mafiya*. I've heard my dad speak of them, but I've never seen them before. Still, there's no doubt in my mind that's who these men are.

I fly to my sister's side, behind the protection of her butcher knife. Our mother doesn't even come out of her room.

"Grigor. Where is he?" one of them demands. They're looking for our father. I know he does business with the bratva. I'm not sure what kind. Maybe that's where he gambles.

"Wh–why? What has he done?" I ask.

"He owes us, and we've come to collect."

"Well, he's not here," Anya says.

One of them advances. His upper lip curls. I don't like the way he's looking at my bare legs. At my sister's breasts. "*Where?*"

"We don't know!" Anya spits. "He's been gone for two days."

"Take the older one," a man says quietly. He must be the leader because the men surge forward to obey.

One of them puts a gun to my forehead, but he speaks to my sister. "Come nicely or your little sister's brains will cover the floor."

Anya, shocked into submission, lets another man take the knife from her hand and grasp her firmly by the upper arm.

"You can't take her!" I'm not begging, I'm shouting. As if I have any power to persuade them.

"Shut her up," the leader says, and the man with the gun slams the side of it against my head. Everything goes black.

The Gatekeeper

When I wake, Anya is gone.

* * *

Maykl, 13 years old

I stand, pistol shaking in my sweaty hand. My breath rasps in and out in harsh measures. I used this pistol four days ago to kill my own father. It was kill or be killed, but I'm still sick over it. I'm still in shock. I've barely slept in the nights since.

I'm grateful the bratva took care of everything. Got rid of the body. Gave me a place to stay. Put money in my pocket. It was Peter, one of the lower leaders, who gave me the gun in the first place.

"For protection," he said when they were at my father's auto shop, and he saw the bruises on my face.

Now, though—what he's asking of me is too much.

"This is how you prove your loyalty, Maykl. Do you want to join the brotherhood?"

I stare down at the beaten man at my feet. Sweat beads along his greasy blond hairline. His light blue eyes bulge with terror. Breath rasps in and out at a rapid rate. "*Nyet... nyet,*" he pleads.

I do want to join the brotherhood. Rather desperately. I assumed I was already in. I won't survive without them. I'll go to prison for killing my father.

"Take my daughter again! Use her," the man pleads.

"We already tired of her," Peter says.

"The younger one, then."

"It's easy," Peter murmurs behind me. "Just pull the trigger. This guy would sell his own daughters. He is scum."

I stop thinking. I have no other choice. I squeeze the trigger...

And miss.

"Again, Maykl." Peter's patient. "Right between the eyes. You can do it."

The second time, I don't miss. Clean shot in the head.

He dies immediately.

Grigor Koslov. I memorize his name as the ink is pressed into my skin to memorialize the crime.

My first murder on behalf of the bratva.

First of far too many.

Chapter One

Sixteen Years Later

Kira

I stand in the Cook County morgue and stare down at the wasted body of my sister. A wave of nausea rolls through me, even though I prepared myself for this sight. She's skin and bones, reduced to a skeleton long before the final overdose took her. Her arms are covered in needle tracks.

This is the conclusion to yet another life ruined by the bratva. The second family member I've lost at their hands.

I barely slept on the plane from Russia, but seeing Anya's horrific form instantly clears the fog from my brain and brings on an urgent sense of purpose: I need to find my nephew. I came to bring him home with me. It's what I should have done years ago.

I was still in school when Anya left with Mika, but I begged her to leave him with me. I already knew the bright future she fantasized about for them here wouldn't happen.

"That's her," I tell the morgue attendant. I started learning English the day she left with Aleksi, her client. Or boyfriend. Or whatever you call the bratva thug who pays you for sex and treats you like shit.

I suppose I always knew this day would come. I'm grateful now that I can understand and speak English well enough to get by.

"What do you want to do with the body?" The attendant at the morgue asks.

"I...I don't know yet."

"You have twenty-four hours to make arrangements. I'm sorry to rush you, but she's already been here three days, and we need the space here," the sharp-nosed attendant tells me. He's nice enough. He tries to warn me off actually viewing the body and just identify her through a photograph, but I refuse.

I push back the mountain of grief that threatens to crush me. Now is not the time to mourn Anya. I don't have the luxury to grieve yet. And dealing with Anya's body is the least of my worries right now. "Okay. I'll figure it out. Thank you."

My next visit is to the police station to meet with the officer who signed the paperwork when Anya was brought in.

"I'm a police officer, too," I tell him in hopes he'll be more helpful than the one who called me in Russia. I produce my *Politsiya Rossii* identification to show him. "You have no idea where her son might be?"

The graying cop, Officer Green, shakes his head. "The 9-1-1 call came from another female junkie in the crack house where she was living. We haven't investigated, as the cause of death was obviously an overdose."

"May I have the address of the crack house, please?"

"Of course. You say she has a son? How old?"

The emotion that was absent from seeing my dead sister

suddenly floods me at grief for the loss of Mika. My sweet nephew. The boy I bounced, fed, and taught to walk. The child I raised when I was just a teenager.

"He'd be... fifteen now."

"And the father?"

I shake my head. Who knows which bratva *mudak* actually sired Mika. It could have been any one of them who passed her around as payment for our father's debt.

"No father."

A junkie mother. And this kid on his own, living in a foreign land. It's horrible. I've been trying to find both of them since I lost contact with Anya over four years ago, but even with my police ties, I found nothing.

Guilt tightens my gut. I should have done more.

This time, I'll make it right. I won't leave until I find my nephew.

I work hard to keep the wobble out of my voice. "I've been searching for my sister and nephew for several years. I'd like to file a missing person report on the boy."

"Okay. We can check the database for any information on him, too. See if he's popped up in the system," Officer Green offers. He leads me to his desk where he sits behind a computer to enter the report.

"Thanks."

I already know it won't show anything. I've had a data request on them both for years, which is how they contacted me when they found my sister dead.

Officer Green fills out the missing person report and writes down the address of the crack house.

"Your sister's tourist visa expired years ago. What brought her over here to begin with?"

I draw in a long, steadying breath. "The bratva."

"Russian *mafiya*?"

"Yes."

The cop grimaces. "Could the boy be with them? He's old enough—he might be part of the organization by now."

I nod. "My thoughts exactly, but most of those men turned up dead several years ago in a mass shooting."

Officer Green frowns and nods. "I remember it. Some kind of mafia turf war with the Italians."

"Do you know if any of them survived?"

He shakes his head. "No idea. But the bratva stronghold is down on Lake Shore Drive. They own an entire high-rise building–the neighborhood calls it the Kremlin. You could start there. I understand it's sort of an embassy to any Russian in need, so you might show up and play dumb, you know? Hide that badge of yours and tell them you need a place to stay. I heard they only rent to Russians, and for a subsidized rate." He shrugs. "Just an idea."

I'd rather barge in with a gun in each hand and search every room until I get an answer, but I know I wouldn't last a minute. Officer Green is right. If I want to succeed, I may have to go undercover.

Find Mika and get enough information to tear this whole operation down. If not through the American police, then through the bratva in Russia. I can pit them against one another and incite a war.

"What sort of crimes are they into, do you know? Prostitution? Drugs, I presume?"

Officer Green takes off his police cap and scratches his head. "I'm sure they're into everything, but other than an arson charge last year, they've stayed squeaky clean." He takes the paper he wrote the flophouse address back from me and writes the address for the bratva building and a phone number.

"That's my number. If you find anything worth reporting, call me. Don't put yourself in danger. I know you're a cop and can handle yourself, but I'm sure you understand these men are extremely dangerous. Plus, I should remind you that this isn't your jurisdiction. Any arrests will have to come through my department or the FBI. We clear?"

I nod. "Understood."

He hands the paper back to me. "Good luck."

"I appreciate it." I stand and hold out my hand to clasp his.

His concerned gaze holds mine. I know what he's thinking. What the bratva would do with an attractive woman like me if things went sideways. "Be very careful."

"I'm not afraid," I tell him.

I'll use my beauty to my advantage, if necessary. The way the bratva treats women, they will see me as nothing more than an object, anyway.

I toss my hair out of my eyes. "They should be afraid."

* * *

Maykl

I stand watch behind my desk as strangers off the street wander into our building for Kateryna's open house. Her studio, Kremlin Clay, has a once-a-month open house where she and a handful of other potters sell their wares.

I head up security for our building, so I have men stationed all over the first floor to make sure nothing goes wrong.

My *pakhan*, Ravil, has Leo, a seventeen-year-old Russian-American who lives in the building, serving as a doorman while I keep a close watch on everyone from behind the desk.

"Welcome to the Open House." Leo speaks flawless

English, having moved here as a child. He's not bratva—at least, not yet. He lives in the building with his single mother. Ravil gives him work—at a very generous wage—to help them out. He's not just *pakhan* to the bratva. He considers himself a sort of tribal leader to everyone in the building.

"The studio is just past the elevators on your left." Leo invites in a young couple.

I'm in a suit, my tattoos mostly covered, other than those that crawl up my neck. I try to keep the customary menace and suspicion from showing on my face, while still monitoring their every move.

It's my job to assess danger at this entry point. I'm the gatekeeper. The guy who keeps out all threats to our occupants, especially to our *pakhan*.

Security cameras are on, recording everything. The stairwell doors lock from the outside. No one can take an elevator without a keycard. I see everyone who goes in or out of the restrooms.

Nikolai, Oleg, and Adrian are inside the studio, armed and extremely dangerous.

Still, this level of intrusion into what is normally an impenetrable fortress has me on edge.

Nikolai and Chelle saunter out to the lobby of the building holding glasses of champagne. I notice Nikolai's drink appears untouched. He may appear casual, but he's on duty like I am.

Chelle sets a small plate of hors d'oeuvres on the counter for me. "Nikolai said no alcohol for you, but I brought you some snacks."

I clear my throat trying not to look too grateful because Nikolai, who is normally laid-back, gets irrationally jealous of his fiancée. "Thank you."

"How many have come through?" Nikolai asks, knowing I will have an exact tally in my head.

"Forty-nine in, twenty-two out," I report.

Chelle looks disappointed. She's a publicist with the top publicity firm in the city, and she arranged a social media blitz to advertise tonight's open house. "Well, there's still another hour."

Personally, I think there are plenty in attendance. More than I like having to keep track of.

"There's hardly anything left in there to buy," Nikolai consoles, his hand possessively at Chelle's back.

Though they've been together a few months, I'm not used to this domesticated version of Nikolai. Nor of any of my brothers who are now paired with a woman.

Ravil's break with the bratva code of forbidding marriage and relationships seems more dangerous than anything else he's done.

Seeing my brothers paired up, seeing them in love, leaves me cold. I've already seen how irrational the women make them. How the females cloud their judgment and affect their decision-making.

Most of all, it creates some kind of scratchy void deep inside me. A prompting to wonder what it would be like for me to claim a woman. To have someone soft and beautiful warming my bed.

Not that I don't bring a woman home on occasion. I get my basic sexual needs met. But finding a partner–that's something different.

The mere idea of it creates unease in me. A noisy clamoring of danger.

I'm sure it's related to some basic primal wound of having my mother abandon me at a very young age. Who could blame her? My father was a monster.

But I've never known why she didn't take me with her.

Chelle walks over to praise Leo and asks him how he's doing while Nikolai leans against the counter and eats one of the toothpicks loaded with fancy olives from my plate.

"You hate this, don't you?" Nikolai asks me as Maxim and Sasha join us.

"Every second," I confirm.

"So do I." Maxim's watchful gaze sweeps the newcomers. He, of all of us, hates outsiders in the building most. His wife, Sasha, is the daughter of Igor Antonov, the now-deceased Moscow *pakhan*, who arranged her marriage to Maxim before his death last year. She inherited his interest in oil wells worth over sixty million dollars, which put her in the crosshairs of every *mudak* who dreams of taking her black gold from her. Igor chose Maxim to be her husband, deeming him the best able to protect her.

Maxim will probably spend the rest of his life anticipating threats to her safety.

"But we do these things to make life as normal as it can be for the women. As much as I'd prefer to keep them locked in the penthouse and never let out."

Sasha chuckles and wraps her arms around him and kisses his cheek. "Such gallantry."

Maxim's lips curve. "I try."

Chelle returns to Nikolai's side, and the two couples head back into the pottery studio. As I watch them retreat, I try to ignore the niggle of jealousy that fills me every time I see one of my happily-married brothers with his wife.

* * *

Kira

The crack house is exactly what the name suggested.

The Gatekeeper

It's in a decrepit neighborhood. A side of America I didn't know existed. Streets are littered with garbage. Ramshackle buildings are covered with graffiti. The front windows are boarded up at the address Officer Green gave me. I climb the steps, which are littered with cigarette butts, trash, and a couple of hypodermic needles. I bang on the door. When no one answers, I try the handle. It opens.

There are people inside. It smells of stale smoke and rank bodies. There are several dirty mattresses littering the floor, and trash covers every other inch of it. Someone sits up on the couch. A woman, I think. Her matted hair falls in her face. She's nothing but skin and bones like Anya, her eyes hollowed out and dark.

"Who the fuck are you?" She reveals rotted, stained teeth when she speaks.

"My name is Kira Koslova."

"Another Russian." The woman lurches to her feet, staggering when she arrives. She ignores me, searching the floor for something.

"Did you know my sister? Anya?"

"You got a cigarette?"

"No. Did you know Anya?"

She shoots me a disgusted look. "Yeah, I knew her. She's dead."

"I know. I came from Russia when the police called."

"So? What do you want?"

"I'm looking for her son, Mika. Is he here?"

The woman stops searching the floor and swivels. "She didn't have a son."

My hands clench into fists. A white-hot rage floods my chest, heats my face. It's irrational, but potent just the same. "She did," I snarl. "He'd be fifteen now. *Her son.*"

"No. No son. I've known her a long time. She never had

a son."

Panic flares, but I try to tamp it down with my anger. "How long?" I speak through clenched teeth. "How long have you known her?"

The addict shrugs. "Few years." She shakes her head with a sneer. "Definitely no son."

I want to attack the stupid addict and tell her she's wrong. I want to scream. To throw things. Burn down this wretched building.

But none of those things will help me find Mika.

If I were honest, I'd recognize that the person I'm really angry at is myself. For not stopping Anya from leaving. For not insisting Mika stay with me.

If I hadn't had my heart broken so many times by Anya. If I hadn't been angry with her for the kind of mother she was, for her addiction and her continued association with the men who'd ruined her, if I hadn't given up on Anya, maybe she'd be alive right now. Mika wouldn't be missing. The idea that he may be completely lost to me terrifies me. I have absolutely no way of knowing if Mika's alive or dead. Where to begin to find him. What happened to him.

But that guilt is far too painful. It's easier to blame the bratva. They started this road to destruction by taking Anya as payment. A few months later, they killed our father, anyway.

It's time I figure out how to pay them back for the evil they bestowed on my family.

I get back in my rental car and program the map for the address of the bratva stronghold. Then I dial the number of my supervisor in Moscow.

"Koslova," Stepanov answers. He's an adequate boss. Fatherly. He made a play for me once but backed off when I shot him down. "You okay?"

"No, sir. My sister is dead, and there's no sign of my nephew. He's missing."

He blows out a breath. "I'm sorry," he says gruffly. "I know you were hoping to bring him back with you."

Tears smart my eyes. "I should have come years ago." I don't know why I'm confessing this stuff to Stepanov. He's not the touchy-feely type. Police don't generally do emotions with each other, but the sense of grief and desperation keeps growing. The helplessness.

"The bratva did this," I say bitterly.

"Yes," Stepanov says. "I have heard the Chicago bratva are the worst of them."

I digest that, a fresh surge of anger piercing my grief. "They have a building here where supposedly all Russians are welcome. I'm going there now."

"I've heard of it. It's supposed to be a fortress. If you can penetrate its defenses, much could be done to bring down this American arm of the bratva."

"What do you mean?"

"I have contacts in America–FBI. They have been looking for someone on the inside. They might be willing to help you find your nephew if you can help them."

"Help them, how?"

"You get in that building. Make friends."

My phone interrupts the call to give me the next direction, and I make the required turn.

When the sound changes back to the call, Stepanov has ended the call.

It doesn't matter, I already feel far less alone. Less desperate.

I'll have Stepanov and the FBI behind me on this venture.

All I have to do is get myself in.

Chapter Two

Maykl

Someone's buzzing the bell of the Kremlin front doors. Technically, not my problem. The doors are locked—it's past business hours. It's approaching nine at night, for fuck's sake.

But I have the video feed running in my room because I take security at the Kremlin very seriously, and this one doesn't look like she's going away.

She's holding a suitcase and is hunched against the wind. The long red woolen jacket wrapped around her doesn't disguise how slender she appears. How lovely.

She raises her gloved hand and raps on the glass. "*Pozhaluysta.*" I can't hear the word, but I see her lips form it.

Blyad'. She's Russian.

I'm up and out of my chair in a heartbeat, palming a pistol that I tuck in the waistband of my jeans. I shove my feet in a pair of boots and get on the elevator to go down to the front doors.

I see my share of crazy shit here. I saw when that band

kid tried to knock the doors down a month ago to get in. I knew he was here for Nadia, and I also knew Adrian wouldn't approve, so I didn't even bother answering the door.

As it turned out, Nikolai let the kid in.

I've had to field an aggressive visitor for that *mudak*, too. Before she was his girlfriend, Chelle nearly climbed me like a tree when I tried to throw her out. I guess her brother has a gambling problem that Nikolai helped her out with.

I open the door and stare at the pale beauty looking up at me. Her eyes are ice blue, and her lashes and brows a light blonde.

She takes in my tattoos and the width of my shoulders. "I am Russian," she says in our mother tongue, ducking her head submissively. "I was told I would be welcomed here."

Fuck.

I grunt and open the door to at least let her in from the cold. "Told by whom?" I demand in Russian.

She gives a name I don't recognize.

"What do you need?"

She pulls off her winter cap, revealing a head of pale blonde hair that falls in layers to her shoulders. I get the feeling the submissive act is just that–an act. There's a steely determination behind her eyes that makes me cautious.

"My name is Kira. I just arrived from Russia, and I need a place to stay."

I consider her for a moment. *Nyet*. There's something off about this.

I jerk my thumb toward the door. "So find a hotel." I speak in English to see if she understands me.

Her pale brows draw together, but she replies in accented English. "I can't stay here? Just for a few days until

I get a job and find my bearings?" She unbuttons her coat, and I take in her slender but feminine form. She's in pants that hug her hips and a pair of lace-up boots that give her a mildly punk look. Her sweater is asymmetrical, falling off one shoulder and molding to her perky tits.

She appears alert. In command of herself. She's taken in the opulent lobby as well as the gun at my waist without any apparent surprise. Like she expected as much.

Her gaze travels from my face, to my chest, and down my tattooed arms. When she sees the tattoo that marks me with the sin of patricide, her lip curls slightly with what appears to be distaste. Like she knows what it means.

I narrow my eyes. "What are you really here for?"

She goes still for a moment then draws in a breath and lets it out. "I came to Chicago to find someone. But... it seems they may be harder to locate than I expected. I need a place to stay, and I don't know the area. I can pay a little. Or I could work it off."

I relax a bit because I recognize the note of truth in her voice. Or maybe her demeanor.

She wasn't being suggestive when she offered to work it off, but my mind jumps to all the jobs I'd love to give her.

On her knees, at my feet.

In my bed.

Maybe some light cleaning while she's scantily clothed.

Blyad.' My mind isn't normally this clouded by sex. Something about this waif of a warrior in front of me has me dying to conquer her.

"I heard back home that this place is a bratva stronghold but safe for someone like me." She holds my gaze with hers, and I picture her tied to my bed while I go out and slay dragons for her.

The fact that she admits she knows what we are relaxes

me even more. That was the vibe I got. She didn't just wander in off the street. She understands we are a criminal organization. Dangerous—but not to her. It explains her demeanor. But where is she from? How does she know about us?

These are problems that need to be solved before I just let her into the building.

I consider her.

Her beauty does strange things to my decision-making skills. Something about that bowtie mouth. The exquisite bone structure. The egg-shaped birthmark on her cheek that looks like a fairy's kiss.

She seems both fragile and strong at the same time.

I can't tell if I'm uneasy because I know something's off about her or because of my dick's reaction. I'm dying to throw her over my shoulder, carry her to my apartment and spread those legs. Find the juicy pink heart between them and feast until she screams.

And that's how I arrive at the answer. The wrong one, I'm certain.

"The apartments are not mine to rent out, but you can stay with me tonight until I can take you to my *pakhan*."

She swallows like she's afraid of what that might mean, but she bobs her head. "Thank you…" She lifts her brows as she holds out her hand.

I clasp it. Her grip is firm, her skin soft. "Maykl."

"Maykl." She gives me the glimmer of a smile.

Seeing that softness on her makes me want to learn her secrets. Earn a full smile. An easy one.

I lock the front doors and reset the alarm then pick up her suitcase. I tip my head toward the elevator. "Let's go."

* * *

The Gatekeeper

Kira

Maykl is gruff but not a *mudak*. Not like the bratva men Anya serviced. They were less civilized than this guy appears. Unintelligent. Certainly not chivalrous. I'm not the type who needs a man to carry her suitcase, but I admit it feels nice.

But that doesn't mean I find Maykl any less dangerous or menacing.

I know what his tattoos mean. The black X's across his knuckles signify his kills. The apple shoved down a tree's throat means he killed his own father. That one is shocking but also not entirely surprising. Most men get into the bratva young. They are street kids, usually with bad home situations. The bratva lures them in with the illusion of glory. The promise of power. They indoctrinate them into manhood through violence and crime.

He leads me to an elevator, which requires a keycard to start.

High-tech. That's interesting. Clearly, this American branch of bratva is swimming in money to be able to afford this kind of stronghold right on the shore of Lake Michigan. I don't know Chicago, but it's obvious this is prime real estate, and the building is new and luxurious. The brass edging and handrails in the elevator gleam. Everything smells fresh and clean and expensive.

We get off on the third floor, and Maykl stomps with his untied boots to a door where he uses his keycard again. It shouldn't be too hard to steal that card from him and have a look around. He's the doorman. He seems in charge of security for the building–a gatekeeper of sorts. I wouldn't be surprised if his particular key opens everything.

Whatever I imagined or expected this place to be is very

far from what I found. It's not some kind of crack house for Russians. It's a beautiful, modern, high-tech fortress.

Which means sleeping with Maykl–I mean, in his apartment–is probably the luckiest break I could have. I'd probably be smart to seduce him to really win his trust and ensure I can stay.

That's not my specialty, but honestly? With Maykl it probably wouldn't be a hardship. He's over six feet of solid muscle, wide across the chest, chiseled in the arms. Any guy who carries a woman's suitcase can't be a total prick in bed. He at least has some level of consideration for others.

Not a total sociopath like the bratva men I've known.

His apartment is small but clean and elegantly appointed. It's open concept with a granite countered peninsula separating the kitchen area from the living room. One wall features a desk with a half-dozen monitors that each display several different video feeds, including one of the front doors.

So that's how he knew I was out there ringing the bell.

He kicks his boots off by the door, so I do the same, shrugging out of my woolen coat.

"Would you mind if I took a shower?"

I don't actually need the shower, but it's part of my seduction act. Again--I'm not an expert with this particular game—that was Anya's gig. But getting naked and wet has to be a step in the right direction.

Maykl lifts his chin in the direction of the bedroom and follows me in with the suitcase, flipping on the light. He has a giant, king-sized bed in the center. It's rumpled like I got him out of it to answer the door. There's a dresser against one wall and two end tables. Otherwise, it's pretty basic. It smells like him–of leather and aftershave and that uniquely masculine scent I caught when we were in the elevator together.

I purposely don't take my suitcase or any change of clothes into the bathroom. That way I can come out in a towel. Maybe accidentally drop it.

As it turns out, the shower is amazing. The stall is a beautiful walk-in with white marble or quartz walls and small iridescent glass tiles on the floor in blues and greens. The showerhead is large, and the spray of warm water is powerful.

I must be more aware of my body from thinking about having sex with the gatekeeper because everything feels so sensual. I bite back a moan of pleasure as I step under the water. It feels so good.

I spend a long time under the spray. He has a razor in there for his face, and I use it to clean up my bikini area and shave my legs and armpits. I wash and condition my hair. Soap every crack and crevice.

All right, maybe I'm stalling.

What if I don't know how to seduce a man? I'm usually the one being hit on, not the other way around.

I close my eyes and channel Anya. After her initial trauma, she learned to claim power in what she had–which was only her body. She was forced into the role, but after that, she embraced it. Learned how to make it work for her. Of course, she had to because after our father was murdered by the bratva four months later, our mother stayed in bed for the next three years.

I think Anya truly believed she was bettering her life and Mika's when she came to America with her bratva boyfriend.

I turn off the water and towel dry then walk out of the bathroom as I squeeze the towel around my hair.

Maykl's not in the bedroom. I walk into the living room where I find him on the couch, his feet propped on the coffee table, watching television. He pauses the show when he sees me but otherwise doesn't give me the reaction I expected.

His eyes narrow as he takes in my nudity. "Kira."

I cock a hip. The tail of the towel falls across one breast. I pretend to be completely unaffected by my state of undress. "I don't mean to keep you from your own bedroom," I say in a soft voice.

He picks his feet up from the coffee table and rises. "Are you trying to seduce me?" There's a note of danger in his voice. A reminder that I'm playing a game that could have life-threatening consequences.

I'm glad Stepanov is waiting for me to check in. If I don't call or text, he will know to send his FBI contacts in after me.

Maykl advances on me. His sheer size and bulk make it hard to hold my ground. Especially naked and without a weapon. I drop the towel completely. I'm already too far in this to not be bold. "Is it working?"

He stops inches from me. Looks down at me from a power stance. "No." The word is no more than a growl, but I notice his pupils are dilated like he's turned on.

He catches me around the throat but doesn't squeeze. His narrowed eyes search my face. "What are you up to, little warrior?"

I would expect my fight instinct to come into play. I'm trained at hand-to-hand combat. I excel with a firearm. But something about Maykl's loose hold around my throat feels far more sexual than threatening.

Like he's showing me how he'd be in bed. Dominant.

Attentive. Gentle when he needs to be. Rough when he doesn't.

Moisture leaks between my legs. My nipples stiffen to tight buds. His gaze dips to one of them, and he brushes the backs of his knuckles over it.

"I'm just"–I draw in a sharp breath when he takes my nipple between his knuckles and squeezes–"showing my gratitude."

He shakes his head. "No. You want something. What is it?"

I know the secret to a good lie is to stick as closely to the truth as possible. That's what I'd done in the lobby when he was quizzing me, and it seemed to work.

"I don't have any resources available to me here. No network. No contacts. I can't afford to stay in a decent hotel for more than a couple of nights." I lift my gaze to his and hold it. "I'd much rather stay here. I'm making friends."

"So you thought you'd suck my dick, and we'd be friends?" he shakes his head. "Sorry, little warrior. I'm not that easy to play."

"You haven't had my mouth on your cock yet."

Chapter Three

Maykl
Blyad'.
A surge of lust makes my fingers reflexively tighten at her throat.

"You're confident."

She nods and starts to lower to her knees, but her jaw catches at my immovable grip.

She wants to suck my cock. It's a trick, obviously. Or a manipulation. Still, she's a goddess with that moon-pale hair and the dark coral bow-tie lips. I want to fuck that pretty mouth if for no other reason than to get something honest out of her.

I know it's the wrong move. It's almost like I can sense the utter destruction this female will rain down on my life, but I also suspect the demise would be worth it. I release my hold on her neck and let her kneel in front of me.

She opens the button on my jeans and frees my erection.

I'm somewhat mollified to see her fingers tremble as she

reaches to grip my length. She's not as practiced at this as she pretends. And she *is* up to something.

She lifts my cock to trace the vein that runs on the underside, from base to tip.

I shudder at the pleasure of it. At my need for more.

I should put a stop to this. Grab her by the arms and haul her to her feet. Slap that pretty ass and tell her to stop her games.

But I've already allowed her to start. I might as well receive the pleasure that precedes whatever wicked destruction I've unleashed at her hands.

She takes the tip of my cock into her mouth and slides it in and out, teasing me. Torturing me.

I grip the back of her head and shove in deep. Remind her who's in charge here.

She stiffens, but recovers quickly, hollowing her cheeks to suck hard as I pull back, then taking me deep toward the back of her throat when I press in again.

"You look so pretty with those lips around my cock," I murmur.

I'm not usually much of a talker–dirty or otherwise–but something about this woman seems to remove all my filters. All my reason.

I caress her cheek with my thumb as my fingers at the back of her head urge her forward and back at a rhythm that has me sucking in my breath through flared nostrils. Relishing the sensation.

Maybe it's because this is wrong. Because I know it's a mistake. Maybe it's because Kira is my own special Kryptonite. Whatever the reason, it *is* the best blowjob I've ever had. She was right. There's something about seeing my little Valkyrie kneeling at my feet, her pale skin flushed with passion, her ice-blue eyes looking up at me for my reaction that unleashes a lust I didn't even know I was capable of.

I shove deeper, hitting the back of her throat and gagging her with my cock. She struggles to take me. When her fingers tighten around the base of my cock, perhaps to control my movements, it only drives my need for her.

I know I'm toeing the line, or, maybe, I've already crossed into disrespect, and somehow, surprisingly, that's what brings my control back. I pull out of her mouth, and in one smooth motion, haul her from her knees to my shoulder. I clap one heavy hand down on her perky ass as I carry her into my bedroom.

When I toss her on the bed, there's a mixture of fear and excitement in the flush of her skin, the whites of her eyes. The way she watches me as I shuck my clothes. Her gaze travels over my hairy chest, taking in the tattoos that cover my right pectoral and shoulder.

She may have been offering the blowjob as a transaction, but I'm all in now. Ready to reciprocate. Dying to see how she looks in the throes of an orgasm.

I climb on the bed and push her knees wide. "I need to taste *you* now, Kira."

"*Oh.*" She sounds startled. Like she doesn't know how to receive my offering. Like it hasn't been done enough to her.

I intend to change that. Show her what she's been missing. The moment I lick into her, her hands are at my ears. I suspect it's more out of a need for control than out of passion. She jerks with every flick of my tongue like it's too intense. More sensation than she's used to.

I pin her hands by her sides. Her knees flap in against my shoulders, squeezing hard.

I lift my head, licking her juices from my lips. "What's wrong, *Valkiriya*? Not used to receiving?"

The stain of dark pink on her cheeks tells me I'm right.

"Do I need to tie you down to help you let go?"

I see the flicker of alarm in her gaze, even though her nipples stiffen into long peaks. She's not experienced at this game she's playing. Not at all.

She pushes up to her elbows. "Wh-why don't you let me finish you?"

Now I'm determined. I'm going to teach her how to receive pleasure.

I climb off the bed and pull my only silk necktie out of the dresser drawer. I walk back to her, stretching it long between my two hands.

"Wrists," I say gruffly.

She doesn't move. There's a glint of defiance in her gaze.

I cock my head. "What's wrong?" I mock softly. "Afraid you bit off more than you can chew?"

That's all it takes. She's competitive, this one. Doesn't shrink from a challenge. With a haughty toss of her damp locks, she holds her wrists out to me.

I wrap one loop around them first to protect her skin, then tie a tight knot. I secure the other end to the headboard. Once she's bound, I stand back and admire my lovely captive.

It's the dichotomy of energies she gives off that makes her so fascinating to me. The waif-like warrior. The seductress soaked in innocence. Now, she looks at me with fluttery anticipation mixed with warning.

She's prepared to take off my head if I fuck this up.

I give her a wicked grin. "Don't worry, I'll make it good, Kira." I cock my head. "Is that even your real name?"

The Gatekeeper

She yanks against the knots like she just realized she might be in trouble. She stops when she sees my smile and lifts her chin. "Yes, it's my name." There's a note of challenge in her voice that makes me believe her.

"Let's just see." I pick up her purse from the dresser and root through to find her passport. Kira Koslova. She's from Moscow, same as I am. I lift my gaze to study her again. I search through the rest of her purse and wallet for anything revealing but find nothing.

I've given her long enough to miss me. To grow needy. I've reminded her who's in charge. That her pleasure comes at my whim.

It's time now to go back to my lovely captive.

I return to the bed where I grip her just above the knees so I can hold her open. I lower my head between her legs and start with a slow torture. A subtle delving of my tongue into her folds. Tracing around her clit. Around her entrance. Around her back hole.

She thrashes and pants. Her muscles squeeze and release. Her ass clenches and shivers. Her belly shudders in and out with each breath. I grow more aggressive, using the flat of my tongue to cover more area at once. I suck her labia, push the hood of her clitoris back to get my lips over the little nubbin.

She's sensitive. Responsive. Her panting breath turns to little mewls and cries. She yanks and tugs against my tie around her wrists. Her legs push against my grip. She lifts her core to my mouth. I penetrate her with my tongue.

I replace it with one finger. Then another. I stroke her inner wall with my fingertips, slowly at first. As her breath grows louder and faster, I shove them in and out, fingerfucking her as I flick my tongue over and around her clit.

I lift my head to watch her face as I thrust into her with

my fingers. Her pale skin is so translucent it shows her flush like bright red slaps, making the fairy's kiss on her cheek blend in.

I remove my fingers, loving her look of shocked disbelief that I would stop before she finished. I grip her pelvis and flip her to her belly, causing her to adjust her bound wrists to get comfortable. Her back is bowed now, her hair turning lighter now as it dries in a fine spray across her shoulders. She's slender but has muscular definition like she works out. I imagine she's stronger than she appears. Of course, she'd be no match for me. I'm twice her weight and a foot taller.

I slide my fingers over her juicy opening, rewarding her for the change of position. Stroking until she humps the bed, moaning plaintively for more. That's when I lift my hand and give her ass a hard slap.

She whirls and glares at me over her shoulder. I slap again—and again. I deliver a dozen blows, turning her ass the same pretty shade as her face.

Then I slide two fingers inside her as my thumb comes to rest on her back hole.

"Have you been fucked back here *Valkiriya?*" My voice is a low, deep growl. I hardly recognize it. I hardly recognize myself. I'm not usually so disrespectful with a woman. Not usually so aggressive and rough.

Somehow, though, it feels right. Like she needs this. Like she deserves it—but as a reward —not a punishment.

"Don't." There's a note of warning in her voice. Forbidding. It makes my dick hard.

I won't. Of course, I wouldn't ever force a woman to do something she didn't want. But it makes me want to bring her to the place where she wants it. Where she begs me for it.

I lower my body over hers as I push my fingers into her sopping channel. *"Nyet?* How about here?" I rumble. "Can I fuck you here?"

"Yes." There's only a second's hesitation.

I try to tamp down the surge of satisfaction at her answer. "I'll use protection," I promise, in case that concern was on her mind. I reach for the bedside stand and grab a condom from the drawer there.

She rolls herself onto her back while I'm away, trying to regain some level of control, no doubt. I unwrap the condom and hold her gaze as I roll it on, watching her eyes darken. The rise and fall of her chest. Her breasts fall open to the sides. She has another red birthmark–a slightly larger one on her ribs. I kiss it first. Then the one on her cheek.

"Fairy's kisses," I say when I notice she's tensed. "I like them."

"Untie me," she murmurs, parting her legs for me.

"Not yet, *moya malen'kaya valkiriya*. You look too pretty like this."

I position myself between her legs and rub the head of my sheathed cock over her entrance. She's wet enough that I slide in easily enough. Her muscles clench around my dick, making me groan.

Her belly hollows and lifts. She watches me, dragging her lower lip through her teeth.

I brace one hand on the headboard and use the other to hold her in place for my thrusts. She rocks up to meet them, taking me deep. Sweet little sounds leave her lips. *Uhns* and *ahs* that grow louder as I work us both into a frenzy.

"Do you like to be ridden hard, little Valkyrie?"

Her blonde brows lower. Nostrils flare. Her breath rasps in and out like she's running a race.

"Or is this the first time you've had it rough?"

I know I'm right when she throws her head back, arching those pretty tits toward the ceiling.

"Beautiful," I mutter. I drag my hand down her throat to squeeze her breast roughly then catch her shoulder before her head bumps into the headboard.

I untie her wrists because the moment for surrender is past. She's already well into it with me, as needy and desperate as I am. Not holding back.

It was the right move because she reaches for my chest, sliding her hands over the planes of my muscles like she was dying to touch me. She grips my arms and scores me with her nails. Wraps her legs behind my back and urges me deeper. Harder.

The bed knocks against the floor. Bangs the wall.

"Come for me, Kira." I pinch one of her nipples, probably too hard.

She cries out, her internal walls squeezing and closing around my cock.

I don't release the nipple, and her eyes fly wide to my face like she's trying to figure out what I'm doing. My own orgasm rushes me forward like a wave of heat pouring down the back of my head to the base of my spine.

Cum surges down my shaft.

"Come harder," I growl and release her nipple at the same moment I climax.

She comes again, clinging to me, no doubt to reduce the roughness of my erratic, ecstasy-laden thrusts.

Fireworks go off behind my eyes, and then I lose all track of what's happening until I find myself covering her body. Crushing her, probably. My sweat mingled with hers. My heart beating against her soft breasts.

The Gatekeeper

I nuzzle into her neck and nip her skin before lifting away. "Are you okay?"

She blinks glassy eyes at me. She appears dazed.

"Did I hurt you, little warrior?"

She shakes her head, a stunned expression still giving her a startled look. Like she didn't know sex could be like that.

Like she's never had it that way or even knew it was possible.

"More than you bargained for?"

"A little." She lets out a soft laugh, almost like she didn't mean to admit it.

I kiss the fairy blotch again and crawl off to dispose of the condom and wash up. I bring her a cool washcloth, which she holds between her legs as if to soothe the area.

I move it aside and kiss her softly there. Light kisses. An apology for being so rough. For leaving her sore.

"I can sleep on the couch," she murmurs softly but doesn't move.

I slide into the bed beside her. "You're not going anywhere." I wrap an arm around her waist and pull her back against my front.

I don't mean to fall asleep so quickly, especially not with a woman I don't trust in my bed, but the orgasm was too strong. Too satisfying.

It's all right, though, because I have this little vixen where I need her. She's not going anywhere without me knowing it.

* * *

Kira

My body trembles from Maykl's rough but expert handling.

My initial assessment of him was correct–he's an experienced and nuanced lover. Dominant and demanding yet still attentive. Gives as much as he takes. I didn't like being tied up, at least not while it was happening, but I now recognize what it did to my body. How it freed me. Let me surrender to the pleasure instead of trying to control it. Or perform. Or whatever it is I usually do with a partner.

I don't even know anymore.

What just happened in this bed is so far removed from everything I've done before. It was so base. Animalistic. Natural. Frightening but also immensely satisfying. One hundred times more satisfying than any other sexual encounter I've had.

But now I'm in a pickle.

Maykl's heavy arm holds me pinned against his body.

I need to get out of this bed and let Stepanov know I'm in. Find out if he's made contact with the FBI.

Part of me–the sexually satisfied part–says I should stay in the warm bed. Fall asleep with this big, burly man. Play a long game with him. Win his trust. Enlist his help. Pump him for information I can use.

But then I remember how suspicious he was of me. How I didn't fool him for a second. From the moment I walked in those front doors, he knew I was up to something. Sensed me as a threat. I'm glad I hid my police identification in the lining of my purse before I came here.

Because he's right.

I am a threat.

I came here to find my nephew, and I don't mind if I tear down their entire organization while I'm at it.

The Gatekeeper

If I'm completely honest with myself, I'd admit that finding Mika feels difficult.

The fact that Anya didn't have Mika with her is deeply troubling. She turned out to be as terrible a parent as our father, which makes me sick to my stomach. And maybe because I need someone to blame, fuels a fierce determination to bring down the organization responsible for ruining her life.

I don't know if I'll find Mika here, but if I can do some damage before I leave, give the FBI something to take them down, I intend to do it.

I have to do something. The bratva killed my father and destroyed my sister's and nephew's lives. In this country, there is supposedly a better justice system than in mine. I intend to use it.

I wait until Maykl's breath has slowed and then pretend I'm just changing position. I roll to face him, moving away from his grip on me and tucking my knees up between us to make space. He stirs when I do, shifting to place his heavy hand on my elbow.

I was right.

He wasn't cuddling. He was keeping me captive in his bed.

Once more, I wait until his breathing slows, then I wait a little longer.

When I move again, he doesn't stir. I'm able to slip out from under his grip.

My clothes are still in the bathroom, and I don't want to get them, so I grab his t-shirt from the floor and pull it on then carefully extract my phone from my purse and creep into the living room.

I start by surveying the security feed. The rows of monitors split into multiple screens showing views from cameras all over the building. I pull out the chair to sit and study them all. It appears he can view the feed from cameras in the hallways on every floor of the building. There's a parking garage beneath the building that's being monitored.

There's nothing interesting or damning in the feed. No dungeons or prisoners to be seen. Of course not. Only in movies are things so neatly laid out and easy. I'll have to do more detective work to find out if Mika is here.

I open my phone and text Stepanov: *I'm in.*

He calls immediately, and I scramble to silence the phone. I consider stepping out into the hallway to take the call but quickly discard that idea. There are cameras everywhere. Instead, I text back. *I can't talk privately. Text me.*

He responds, *My contacts at the FBI said they can help you locate your nephew if you help them infiltrate the bratva.*

What do they need me to do?

They want bugs installed around the building, particularly in the penthouse suite in the pakhan's office. Think you can get in?

The penthouse suite. That could be a challenge, considering Maykl doesn't trust me. Then again, he said he would bring me to his *pakhan* tomorrow.

Maybe. I made a friend.

Male?

Yes.

Good.

Where do I get the bugs? I ask.

Order food delivered with the Uber Eats app. The bugs will come with the food.

Okay. Don't call or text unless you hear from me.

Right. Delete these texts.

On it.

I delete the texts as I hear a slight movement from the

bedroom. Maykl's large form appears. "What are you doing, little warrior?" There's a dangerous note to his voice.

"Sorry, did I wake you?" I sound breathless. I go into the kitchen and open his cupboard and pull out a glass, then fill it with water. "The jetlag has my clock screwed up."

He says nothing. When I swivel to face him and guzzle down half the glass of water, I find him watching me, brows down, a grim expression on his face.

My excuse is plausible. Hell, it's probably true. At least he didn't catch me sitting at his security desk.

"Do you have anything I can take to help me sleep?"

"No." He's not happy with me. "Come back to bed."

I set the glass down on the counter and follow him obediently to the bed, trying to steady my nerves and calm my breath.

I'm skating on thin ice here. Seducing Maykl may have been a pleasurable diversion for the two of us, but it certainly didn't build any trust between us.

I will have to do a much better job at this if I'm going to get him to bring me upstairs.

We climb under the covers, and I roll to face him. "I wasn't entirely honest with you," I offer. I need to give him more. Give him something he can believe. The truth.

He says nothing.

"My sister's dead. I identified her body at the morgue today. I'm looking for her son, my nephew. I thought he might be here."

Maykl reaches out a long arm and turns on the bedside lamp.

"Who is your nephew?"

"Mika Koslova. He's fifteen."

I watch Maykl's face closely but see no flicker of recognition. He shakes his head slowly, a firm frown in place. "What makes you think he's here?"

"He came to Chicago with the bratva. He and my sister both did. It would have been... eight years ago. I hoped—" I allow my true emotion to show in the tremble of my lips— "I hoped you might have him here."

Maykl shakes his head slowly. "No, Kira. I'm sorry. There's no one here that age, nor have I heard the name. I know everyone in the building."

Real tears seep into my eyes, and a sob clogs my throat. I believe him.

He sees my emotion and cradles my face, lowering his lips to press a kiss to my forehead.

I'm not used to being shown tenderness. I didn't grow up with it, nor have I allowed it in my few and far-between relationships. Under normal instincts, I would push him away. Pull myself together and be stoic.

But I intended to show him something real, and now that I have, I'm wobbling on the edge of losing my footing. My defenses were down, and he slipped in.

And I like it.

That's the dumbest part. I enjoy the feeling of being comforted by this man, just as I enjoyed being tied up by him.

There's something about him that makes me want to surrender a little control. Let him lead.

"What bratva?" Maykl asks, picking up the earlier thread of conversation. "Men in the brotherhood don't keep families."

My tears dry up. The familiar bitterness returns. "They were not a family. The bratva took my sister as payment for a debt sixteen years ago. Left her pregnant and ruined her life. She became their whore to provide for herself and the baby. And me." My stomach churns remembering those years.

Me skipping school to take care of the baby while Anya tried to earn enough money to keep a roof over our heads. There was a constant sense of dread–the fear of something even worse happening to us.

I realize now it was based in love. In protectiveness. Because at the tender age of thirteen, I fell in love with that baby boy, as much as if he'd been my own. And my need to protect him and keep him safe outgrew all other concerns.

So, Anya taking him when she moved to Chicago cut out my heart.

But I had no rights. I wasn't his real parent. I may have thought her an unfit mother–I may have even said those words to her–but they made no difference. In fact, I made everything so much worse by driving a wedge between us.

Maybe she would have called me for help sooner if we hadn't parted on such bad terms.

I believe I catch a look of recognition in Maykl's expression–whether it's because he knew my sister or because such behavior is familiar to him, I can't be sure.

All he says is, "I'm sorry."

We lie in silence for a few moments, and then I say, "So can I stay here with you? While I deal with my sister's funeral arrangements and make inquiries about Mika?"

He hesitates then nods. "You may stay with me."

"Do you need your *pakhan's* permission?"

He rubs a hand across his mouth. "Perhaps not. If you're staying with me, and it's temporary."

I nod. "Thank you."

He turns out the light.

I speak again. "Should I speak with him?" I still have to

get myself into the leader's penthouse. "I mean, may I? To ask about my nephew?"

"*Da.* I will bring you tomorrow."

The tightness in my chest eases by one notch. A small victory.

I can plant the bugs, and the FBI will get what they need to bring the bratva down. Then they will help me locate Mika.

Things might work out for me after all.

Chapter Four

aykl

Kira's groggy in the morning–no doubt because her sleep schedule is off–but she rolls out of bed when I do.

After her surrender to me last night–the emotional one, not the sexual–I want to help her. I understand exactly the kind of life she's probably led. I grew up in the bratva, too. Lured from unsavory home conditions into a life of violence and crime. I remember girls like Kira's sister. Brought in to work off debts. Or passed around and given a wad of rubles before being sent home with a slap on her ass.

I understand perfectly why she might show up here thinking she'd find her nephew. Boys like him were often scooped up and incorporated into the brotherhood, just as I was.

All they had to do was rip their very soul from their bodies and pledge the rest of their lives to serve their leader.

I am thankful every day that I don't live in that level of barbarity anymore. That Ravil is a different sort of leader. Here in the Kremlin, I feel like a human being.

Yes, I still use my fists. I still carry a gun. I still see death on occasion. But it all has a reason.

I don't see random cruelty. I don't see sexual slavery or rape, except those women my cell has rescued. Like Nadia, my friend Adrian's sister.

I take a quick shower, and when I emerge, Kira's dressed and sitting on the bed.

She's more subdued today. Less of a Valkyrie. More of a grieving sister. I suppose now that she knows her nephew isn't here, she doesn't have to be prepared for battle.

Seeing her this way makes me want to be the one who goes to battle for her. I pull on my clothes. I need to go and open the building up for business in twenty minutes.

"I ordered us in some breakfast." She holds up her phone. "Uber Eats."

"You didn't have to do that," I tell her. "I have food. But thank you."

She seems surprised by my thanks.

"Where is your sister's body?" I ask. We might as well start with the difficult things. Knock them off her list.

More surprise. Those startled ice-blue eyes find mine. "At the morgue." She swallows. "I was too focused on finding Mika yesterday to make any arrangements."

I nod. "We'll take care of it today."

"*We?*"

I nod. "Wasn't that why you were intent on winning my...*friendship* last night?" I flick my brows, reminding her of her bold act, and she blushes, confirming my suspicion that her clumsy seduction of me was far from her normal behavior.

Now that I understand her background, I can see why she thought it would work. If her sister served as a bratva

The Gatekeeper

whore, she probably thought it was the only currency that works here.

I spread my hands. "You have me now. I want to help."

Her lips part, and she draws in a staggered breath. "Thank you."

"I have to go and open the building for your Uber Eats guy. Do you want to come down with me and wait?"

She stands from the bed. "Yes." She pulls on her boots, and I take her hand to walk her to the elevator.

It's a strange sensation to hold her hand. It feels both familiar and foreign at the same time. Like her hand belongs in mine even though I've never held a woman's hand before in my life.

We ride down in the elevator in comfortable silence. When we get to the door, I see the delivery guy standing there waiting.

I enter the code to disable the alarm then swipe my keycard to open the lock.

I don't like the looks of the delivery guy. He feels wrong. Most delivery guys are slouchy young men, in a hurry to make their drop-off and get to the next one. This guy seems too old. Too solid.

I give him a dark look that doesn't induce him to shrink.

"Uber Eats for Kira?" he grunts, glancing at the receipt. "It didn't have a room number."

"I'm Kira." She reaches for the bag from the nearby bagel shop and flashes him a smile that makes me want to punch the guy's teeth out.

I glower until he leaves, watching until he's completely out of sight.

Kira's already digging through the bag. "If you give me your keycard, I can go and get a couple of plates."

I reach in and take a bagel. "No need. You go up and enjoy. I need to stay at my station for a few hours."

"Okay." She looks so lovely in the morning sunlight, her pale skin set off by those coral lips. Her cornsilk hair swept across her shoulders. I put a knuckle under her chin to nudge it higher and brush my lips across hers.

I suppose I've kissed women before. But the majority of my experience came from the whores back at my cell in Moscow. Never someone I wanted to impress. Or cared about.

So this feels like a first kiss to me.

It's the first time I've had a beautiful woman looking up at me with gratitude. The first time I've expressed my attachment through the bond of our lips. She stills for it. Moves hers softly against mine.

I don't ask for more. It's not the time. We have funeral arrangements to make. She needs to eat. I have to work.

Still, I want another taste. I steal another kiss. A deeper one. No tongue, but my lips slant over hers, sealing my promise to help her.

When I break it, she's leaning into me, her skin flushed with color, eyes brightened in contrast.

"Um. Okay." She gives a breathy laugh. "I'll be in your apartment."

I hand her my keycard. "It's 303," I tell her, in case she didn't take note of the apartment number.

"Yep. I'll be there."

"Good." I ignore the stirrings produced by the thought of having her up in my apartment. The sense of pride it produces. Of possessiveness. Like she belongs to me now.

Which, obviously, isn't even remotely the case.

Besides, I already know what happens when you get attached to a woman, and then she leaves. I'd be a fool to allow myself any feelings when it comes to my lovely warrior.

She's not mine, and she's not staying.

But if I did pick a woman to be mine, it would be one just like her...

* * *

Kira

I dump the bagel bag out on Maykl's kitchen counter. I find a small plastic envelope bundled inside the napkins that contains a dozen tiny listening devices. They each have an adhesive backing, making them easy to stick in the locations I choose.

Things could not go more perfectly.

Opening up to Maykl last night was the right move. If I forget about my embarrassing and obvious attempt to seduce him, I played everything else just right. I'm now totally in with Maykl. I can stay in his apartment. He's going to bring me upstairs to see his *pakhan*.

And on top of that, he seems to want to help me with Anya's funeral arrangements.

Which is...unexpected. And sweet.

A stab of guilt runs through me at my deceit. I'm taking advantage of his kindness.

But the bratva takes advantage of innocents all the time. On a daily basis, I'm sure. I'm sorry because it seems Maykl is one of the few decent ones, but I can't let that stop me from my mission.

The FBI needs intel on the bratva, and in return, they will help me find Mika.

That's all that matters here.

I remove the listening devices from the plastic bag and

drop them loose into my pocket, so they are easy to grab. I have the opportunity to scatter them throughout the building now, but not without first disabling the security feed, and I can't do that while Maykl's on duty. Maybe tonight, after he's asleep. But I'll keep them on me, so if I see an opportunity to plant one, I can.

I give Stepanov a call, even though it's late evening in Moscow.

"Did you get the bugs?"

"Yes, sir. I have them, and I should have the opportunity to plant them in the *pakhan's* office sometime later today."

"Excellent. Good work, Koslova." My supervisor sounds exuberant–almost more enthusiastic with his praise than normal. Maybe he believes impressing the FBI will somehow bring him esteem. "I'm sure with you in that building, they will be able to get all the information they need to bring down the cell. I may fly out myself to facilitate things."

I pause to absorb that. "Really, sir?"

"I don't like the idea of you in there without backup. Even if I can't be in the building with you, I'd like to be available for regular reporting."

Something about that sounds wrong. Is he using this as an excuse to work closely with me? Does he still harbor some kind of interest in me that extends beyond my position?

"They are running your nephew's name through the database now. Their databases are more extensive than the Chicago police department. If your nephew is alive, we should be able to find him now."

For the first time since I arrived in this country, a shred of hope blooms in my chest. "Thank you, sir. That's great news."

"Yes. Listen, Koslova. I expect regular check-ins from you, so I know you're safe. Understand?"

"Yes, sir. I'll check in twice a day."

"Very well. Keep up the good work."

"Thank you, sir."

I end the call and spread cream cheese on a bagel.

They're looking for Mika. Soon, I hope–I would pray if I were the praying type–I'll be reunited with the boy I'd do anything for.

And if I take down one branch of the organization responsible for killing my father, then that's just icing on the cupcake.

Chapter Five

Maykl

aykl

Gleb relieves me of my door duties at ten. He's a seventy-year-old bratva brother with failing lungs, but he's hard as nails. No less dangerous than any of us. Perhaps more so because he's old-school. He came to us this year from a cell in New Jersey.

He and another bratva brother, Dmitri, work under me as doormen, and I have another half-dozen brigadiers I utilize for building security as needed.

I tell him I'll be away for the afternoon, but he should call my cell or notify those in the penthouse if anything happens.

Then I go upstairs to find Kira. When I come in, she's on her back with her toes tucked under the sofa, doing crunches.

"Don't stop," I say when she immediately stops and rolls to her side. "You look beautiful."

"Doing sit-ups?" she scoffs.

"*Da.*" I nod and push away from the door. "I like your warrior side. Female strength is captivating."

She crawls to her feet. "You're crazy," she mutters, but I note the tinge of pink that crawls up her neck. I suspect she likes to be revered for something other than that perfect face.

"Are you ready to go to the funeral home?"

"Uh, yes. But Anya is still at the morgue. I didn't make any arrangements yet."

I nod. "I already contracted with a mortuary. They are on their way to get her now."

She goes still, her lovely chin tilting up. "Thank you." The words are soft with awe like no one has ever been kind to her.

I know how that feels.

It makes me even more determined to come to her aid.

"Come. Let's go." I pick up her woolen coat and hold it out for her to slide her arms in.

It's a gentlemanly action, and I'm no gentleman. I don't even know how this instinct in me arose, yet it feels so natural to honor her this way.

She slides her arms in the sleeves and knots the tie around her waist. I put on a black leather jacket and take her hand in mine to lead her to the elevators.

We take it down to the parking garage, Kira nervously fiddling with the handrail in the elevator as we ride. I lead her to my Ford Bronco and open the passenger side door for her.

Outside, snow has begun to fall in thick, wet flakes that melt when they hit the windshield. The streets are a mess, but I navigate through them, familiar with downtown and the best routes to take.

"Why are you doing this for me?" she cuts through the silence.

The Gatekeeper

I shrug. "I know what it's like to be alone in a strange place."

She gives me a sidelong glance. "You came here alone?"

"Yes, but that wasn't it. Coming here wasn't so hard. Not even learning a new language."

"When, then?"

I don't know what makes me say it. I have this urge to show her that I understand the misery her sister endured, I guess. Even if I didn't suffer like her.

"When I joined the brotherhood. It was...supposed to set me free. But it only further enslaved me to a life of violence."

Now I have her full attention. "Why did you join?"

I shrug. "I was young. My mother abandoned me. Left with me with my abusive father. The bratva put a gun in my hand and told me I could free myself."

Kira's head bows and her gaze drops to her hands. "A common story, I'm sure. The promise of a better life. Power and money and freedom from abuse." She looks over again. "Were you free from abuse?"

I snort. My body is covered in scars from the violence doled out by my brothers and enemies of the brotherhood, alike.

She looks back through the snowy windshield. "Of course not."

We arrive at the funeral home, and I park the Bronco. Kira hops out, and we walk in.

"Ms. Koslova?" The woman at the front desk greets us when we walk in.

Kira looks surprised. "Yes."

"Follow me," the receptionist says, ushering us down a hallway. "The director will be right in to go over the arrangements with you."

She leaves us alone in a room with a large table in the center and backlit glass shelves along two walls displaying all the various options for the dead.

Kira's upper lip curls in distaste as she walks around, looking at the presentation. "You can make gemstones out of a person's ashes? Ew."

"Kira, don't choose based on cost. I'm going to cover the expenses."

"Why?" She almost sounds angry.

"Because I want to. The bratva ruined her life. Paying for her funeral seems like the least we can do."

"Did..." she works to swallow. "Did you know her, Maykl?"

"I knew many women like her," I say in a tired voice.

She nods and turns away, blinking back tears as she picks up a book showing the various casket options and flips through it.

"Do you want to bury her here?" I ask. When she gives me a blank look, I clarify. "In America?"

"Oh." It's like she hadn't considered what a burial would mean. "No." She shakes her head, agitation making her shoulders creep up toward her ears.

"You want the body transported home?"

"No." She appears sickened by the idea. "I guess I want...her ashes."

"So thinking of cremation?" The funeral director enters the room. She's a young woman in a staid, navy-blue suit with an appropriately somber expression.

"Yes."

"Have a seat. I can go over the options and fill out the necessary paperwork."

Ninety minutes later, the arrangements are made. Despite my offer to cover any expense, Kira went with the most basic options. The hundred-dollar cardboard container for the ashes. No service. No remembrances. The entire cost was twelve hundred dollars, which I paid for in cash. Plus another five thousand to get it turned around by tomorrow instead of the two weeks she originally quoted us.

I didn't pay out of guilt. It's not that I feel directly responsible in any way for the woman's demise. But I make good money working for Ravil. I have a very large nest egg. The money is nothing to me, and if I can help Kira move through her grief with more ease, I want to do it.

Especially when Kira gives me a soft "thank you, Maykl" when we get in the car.

I reach for her hand and squeeze it. When she looks over at me with those ice-blue eyes, there's a vulnerability behind them that makes my chest squeeze. Gone is the warrior, and the woman in her place looks lost.

* * *

Kira

It takes me most of the afternoon to recover my footing from the outing to the funeral home. My grief has always been coated in anger. It fuels my strength. Made me join the *politsiya*. Not that I had delusions the police would fix the crime and corruption in my city. I just didn't want to feel weak. I wanted to be able to handle myself. To carry a weapon and wield a little more power than the average citizen.

Something about having Maykl's solid form beside me, feeling like someone had my back for the first time in so many years, made the grief feel more like…grief. Something painful and sticky I couldn't shake.

Maykl took me to lunch after the funeral home then

back to the building. His *pakhan* wasn't available to see me today, so he left me in his apartment while he went back to work an evening shift.

I shower. Work out again in Maykl's living room. Now, I check in with Stepanov.

"Koslova." He answers immediately. "I heard two of the bugs are already online."

"Yes, sir. I placed one in each elevator. Tonight, I will deactivate the security cams and place the others throughout the building. Tomorrow I will see their *pakhan*."

"Excellent work. Tell me about the security system."

I hesitate. Why is my boss so intensely interested in this mission? It's more interest than he ever showed on my cases back home. "Did you decide to fly out here, sir?"

"Yes. I'm en route now."

That takes my breath. "You are?"

"I'll be there by midnight. The FBI are asking for a full description of the layout of the building including exits and entrances, as well as details about the security and HVAC system. They expect trouble when they go in to make arrests and wish to be prepared."

I lean my head against the window overlooking the lake. The idea of a show-down here in this building makes my stomach knot. If that happens, people will die. Many people on both sides.

I shouldn't care, but Maykl could be killed. He's right at their front door. Their gatekeeper. He'd be the first line of defense.

After the generosity he showed me today, betraying his kindness and hospitality doesn't feel like a win. But I didn't come here to make friends. I came to get my nephew and take down the bratva.

Using Maykl is the path to that end goal.

That thought doesn't quiet the discomfort fizzing up my neck, though.

I switch my brain back to business, though. "The locks are all electronic, activated with keycards. There's a keypad at the front door. I believe the code is 87847. I can verify that for certain tonight." I memorized it when I watched Maykl lock up the night I arrived. He'd shielded the screen from my view, but I watched the movements of his finger and, using a mental map of the keypad, guessed at the sequence. "There are cameras above the outside entrance and in every hallway and elevator, but not in the apartments themselves. At least, not that I've seen."

"And you know how to disable the security feed?"

"I know how." My last case involved a breach of a system like this. The expert we consulted with had explained to me exactly how it was done. "Any word about Mika?"

"Not yet, but it's only been a day. They're working on it. Don't worry. They have the resources necessary to locate the boy. How is your *friend*?"

I hesitate. Is Stepanov jealous?

No, that's ridiculous. He's just looking for a full report.

"I appear to have won his trust."

"Good work."

I end the call and, restless, head downstairs. Perhaps I can explore the building before it's dark. Pretending to be turned around for the cameras watching, I take the wrong turn off the elevator and come to what appears to be a retail space.

A sign reading "Kremlin Clay" hangs over the doorway. I try the knob, and it opens.

Inside a young woman dressed in short plaid flannel shorts despite it being winter straddles a spinning pottery wheel. Her wet hands lovingly guide a lump of clay into a bowl shape.

Her dark hair hangs in two long braids. Short bangs frame her eyes. She tosses an easy smile my way. "Hi."

This scene is such a far cry from anything I would ever find in a bratva stronghold back in Moscow that I stop and stare, transfixed.

"Are you lost?" she asks. She speaks English but with an accent that isn't American. I don't know English well enough to identify it. I also don't think it's her native language.

"Oh. Um, yes. I mean, I saw the sign and wondered what was inside."

The young woman keeps molding the clay, pulling the lip of the bowl higher and wider. "You're Russian. Who do you know here?"

"Maykl." I jerk my thumb in the direction of the front desk. "I'm staying with him."

"Are you?" She stops the wheel, and the pile of clay collapses in a disappointing heap. I almost gasp at the loss. "He didn't mention it." She gets up from the wheel. She wears a smock over some kind of adorable rounded-collar fitted blouse. She's sexy in that ingenue way.

She goes to the sink and washes the clay from her hands. I use the opportunity to tuck a bug under one of the cabinets that line the wall.

"I'm Kat. Adrian's girl."

I stare blankly.

"Adrian and Maykl are friends. How do you know him?"

I'm tempted to lie but know that would bite me in the ass. "Oh. Um, we met recently. My sister died, and he's helping me with the arrangements."

The Gatekeeper

"I'm sorry for your loss." Kat walks over and extends her hand.

"I'm Kira," I offer, realizing I hadn't reciprocated the introduction.

"Are you and Maykl…" She lifts her brows.

"Yes," I say but only because I'm playing a role here. Normally, I would deny I had intimacy with any other human.

"Well, it's great to meet you. Welcome to the Kremlin." Her smile is infectious. She's captivating. Nothing about her resembles the kind of women who consort with bratva members in Moscow. Nothing screams drug user. Or sex slave or anyone tortured, used, or owned by the bratva.

On the contrary, there's a vibrancy about her that I've never seen before. It's…stunning. It suffocates me. Like I lived my entire life without realizing that kind of vibrancy was possible. And now that I know, I don't want to crawl back into my own bleak existence.

I sort of hate this beautiful young woman as much as I want to drink in her vitality.

Once again, this anomaly in a bratva-controlled building throws me off my game. Shows me just how little I know about the enemy I've come to infiltrate.

"Are you interested in pottery?"

"I…yes," I say, even though I've never given pottery even a passing thought. It's so far away from my life. "I was fascinated watching you. Please don't let me interrupt. I mean, I know I already have."

Kat laughs lightly. "Do you want to try it?"

"Me? No," I say quickly. I don't like to do things I'm not good at.

"Come on." Kat's smile is warm. "I think you do. It's fun."

She opens a drawer and pulls out a clean smock, which she hands to me. I pull it on over my head and tie the strings in the back, even as my brain protests this insane idea of me trying to make a pot.

Kat leads me back to the wheel. "Have a seat." She hands me the lump of clay that crumpled when she stopped. "Get your fingers wet and make this into a ball."

I dip my fingers in the cup of muddy water and mash the clay. It's more satisfying than I would have expected. Responsive. Easy to mold.

She points at the foot pedal. "You start the wheel down there, and you can control the speed."

"Start slowly," she laughs when I gun it. "Okay, now place the clay right in the center, but keep your hands around it."

She continues to talk me through pressing my thumbs down in the center to part the clay. It wobbles off-center and flops into a blob, and I stop with an embarrassed laugh.

"It takes time," Kat assures me. "No one gets it at first. Hours at the wheel is the only way to learn. Give it another try."

I try a few more times. It's easy to see how it could be addictive.

"You're not Russian?" I make conversation. "I heard only Russians live here."

"I'm from Ukraine. Almost everyone here is Russian, but there are a few exceptions." She flashes a smile at me. "For love."

"Is love allowed in the bratva?" I'm not sure if I'm allowed to mention the brotherhood, but I won't learn anything if I don't push in.

"Not usually." Kat leans a hip against the counters as I

get up to wash the clay off my hands. "When a *pakhan* falls in love, he must change the rules for everyone, no?"

I digest this nugget of information. I still don't even know the *pakhan's* name, but hearing that a ruthless leader has a heart seems out of character. I'm not one to believe in love stories or happily-ever-afters, but it seems love truly can pierce even the blackest of souls.

"So, his girlfriend is not Russian?"

"His wife. No, she's American. There are two other American women here. And me."

"Is it safe?" I find myself asking, even though I'm pushing my luck.

Kat doesn't seem to take offense. "Oh yes. We're very safe. Maykl guards the door, and Dima monitors everything remotely. And it's all very civilized. Nothing illegal ever happens here."

She seems so sure.

Maykl opens the door and steps in.

My body reacts immediately to his presence. His large, imposing form affects me chemically. Everything heats and melts. Relaxes and grows excited at the same time.

"There you are. You cannot roam the building unattended, little warrior."

I immediately go to his side, and he settles a hand on my hip. It's an easy, comfortable gesture. A light claiming. I want to both reject it and lean into it at the same time.

"I'm sorry. I took a wrong turn off the elevator, and then when I saw Kat at the wheel, I was transfixed." Only a partial lie.

He tucks me closer to his side. "It is amazing to see the clay transform in just a few seconds, isn't it?"

Something that resembles pain starts up in my chest. I don't know what it's about. Something related to this man and what he does to me. Finding he can talk about ordinary, artistic things like clay art. That he appreciates such things. That he's not just the violence and crime depicted on his skin.

But I shake it off. Feelings like that are dangerous.

Tonight, I will betray Maykl. Wishing for a different outcome will only make it harder.

Chapter Six

K*ira*

For the second night in a row, I escape the confines of Maykl's heavy arm after having mind-blowing sex and get out of bed. I pull on his t-shirt and pad silently into the living room. There, I disable the security feed from Maykl's screens and stop the recording. The next task is to find Maykl's keycard. I search near the front door. Nothing there.

Bingo. I find it on the kitchen counter.

I need to be back before Maykl moves from deep sleep to REM. I tucked the bugs into the sleeve attached to my phone case earlier and left it in the living room for an easy exit. Now, I pick it up, slip out the door and look for a fire stairwell in case the keycard activations are tracked in the elevator. I find it, snap a photo, and take the four flights all the way down to the parking garage.

There, I find the HVAC system. I snap more photos, showing the entrance, the door to the stairs, the HVAC, and the elevator. I text them to Stepanov, one by one, then delete the texts and the photos from my phone.

There's a keypad on the outside of the door to the stairwell.

I try Maykl's keycode on the door first. It works. I reenter it to re-engage the lock and head upstairs.

The door to the first floor opens right behind the front desk.

I try the code on the keypad to the front doors. It also works. I text Stepanov to tell him.

I take photos of the door, the security cameras, the keypad and send all of them over, careful to erase everything immediately afterward.

Next, I plant a bug beneath Maykl's desk. Then I try the drawers, but they're all locked. He may have information related to the building's security or HVAC system in there.

I search for a paperclip and find one holding a delivery slip to a receipt. I unbend it and drop to my knees in front of the desk drawer. It takes a bit of work, but I get it open.

There's nothing in the drawer, though. I mean, just junk. Random, lost-and-found looking items. Nothing of any importance.

I try the top drawer. It's a little easier to jimmy the lock, but it also contains nothing of interest. Pens. Sticky notes. A few business cards.

The soft tread of a footfall is my only warning before I'm grabbed roughly from behind, one hand clapped over my mouth, an iron forearm at my windpipe. "What are you doing, little Valkyrie?"

I fight back, an elbow to the ribs, a kick to the nuts. I get free and grab the office chair, hefting it as I spin to smash it into Maykl's solid form.

He deflects it with his arm, and it knocks me in the head before it clatters to the marble floors.

I kick him in the gut and run for the door.

I don't even make it a step, though. He catches my wrist, wrenching it behind me until I fall to my knees with a cry.

"Surrender, Kira," he growls. "Your game–whatever it is–is up."

* * *

Maykl

Blyad.' I knew this woman was trouble, and yet I let her in the building anyway. Talked myself into believing she was innocent. What kind of gatekeeper am I?

Shame and anger burn in my throat. Guilt vines around my chest. I've worked hard to make myself useful and trusted to Ravil, our bratva *pakhan*. Serving him is an honor. He's like no other leader in the bratva. He is dangerous, yes, but not evil. Not corrupt. He leads through trust, not fear.

Now I have to go to him and explain I let a woman into our domain despite my better instincts. That I let my dick do the thinking.

I force Kira to stand, pick up the phone she inexplicably brought down here, and frog march her to the elevator, grabbing my key card from her hand.

I took the stairs down when I realized she had left my apartment. I saw her on the video feed crouched behind my desk and didn't want the elevator to alert her to my approach.

"What were you looking for?" I growl after the elevator doors close.

She says nothing.

There's no more pretending we are friends. No more attempts at seduction.

"Who are you, really, Kira Koslova?"

Again, she gives me the silent treatment.

I don't trust her enough to release my hold on her arm even though I know it hurts her. She's been trained to fight. She's not some innocent girl who wandered in off the street. Not that I ever made the mistake of assuming she was. But whoever this woman is, she's capable of holding her own, and I'd be an idiot to underestimate her again.

I turn her and press her against the wall with my fingers choking her breath. "Who sent you?" I demand.

She wheezes.

"Who?"

"Nobody," she chokes out.

I don't believe her, but I release my grip anyway. She was already turning red. My fingerprints stand out on her lovely swan neck.

I hate myself for it, even though it has to be done.

I gather her hands behind her and walk her to my apartment. Now what?

It's the middle of the night. I'm not going to rouse Ravil with this situation. Especially not until I know more.

For some inexplicable reason, I'm reluctant to tell him at all. Not because I fear his anger–although I would hate to face his wrath or even disappoint him.

No, it's more that I can't stand turning her over to my cell.

She requires interrogation. Considering how experienced and unafraid she appears, I suspect she won't spill her secrets easily. Which means torture.

The men of my cell are practiced at the art. Pavel, especially, although he's in Los Angeles now. Adrian can be particularly cruel. They all are steeped in violence, even though you'd hardly guess from appearances now with how soft they seem with their women.

The thought of one drop of Kira's blood spilling on their plastic tarp makes my fingers curl into fists. It brought me physical pain to see the metal leg of that office chair strike her temple. Thank fuck she didn't seem too badly harmed.

I keep her wrists manacled in my hand as I open my desk drawer and pull out a roll of silver duct tape. I wind it liberally around her wrists, securing them behind her back. As I do, the hem of my T-shirt rides up in the back, revealing her bare ass.

My brain stutters. Stops.

Rewinds. She sneaks downstairs to search my desk naked? Or practically naked?

And also: I *fucking love* the sight of her swimming in my shirt.

Before I even think, I have her pinned over my desk, and I spank her ass fast and hard.

It's infinitely satisfying to take out my residual aggression on her gorgeous ass. To deliver my irritation and annoyance at the stunt she pulled without actually harming her.

Because even though I haven't admitted it to myself, I already know the truth: I'm incapable of spilling her blood. There will be no waterboarding. No fingers clipped off or fingernails removed.

I can't allow any of the members of my bratva cell to torture her, either.

Which means I have an even bigger problem: how will I get the information I need from her?

Apart from her initial gasp of surprise, she keeps quiet for the spanking, only shifting her hips right and left and dancing on her feet. I keep at it until I'm mollified. It's not meant to teach her a lesson or anything stupid like that.

It's for my own satisfaction. A way to release my frustration and reward my libido. To remember what she looked like, writhing beneath me just over an hour ago.

I stop and rub her heated skin, my dick growing against my zipper.

I shouldn't. I really shouldn't. But because she's already given herself to me twice, I have this proprietary feeling. Like she belongs to me. Like she's mine to do with as I wish.

So I let my fingertips stray between her legs.

When I find she's wet, I have to grind my teeth to keep back the growl of satisfaction.

But no. Neither of us is going to get relief again tonight. She's my prisoner now.

That thought prompts me to deliver one more sharp slap to her reddened ass.

I push her to sit in one of my straight-backed kitchen chairs where I attach her ankles to the legs. Aw, fuck. Now her knees are parted. That juicy flesh is eye-level, teasing me.

I lift my gaze to hers. Her eyes are wide, those coral lips parted. Her breath trembles in and out at a ragged pace. Of course, she knows what I'm thinking.

Wonders which direction this will go.

I square my shoulders and stand. *Nyet.* She's not my plaything. She's an enemy trying to get past my gates.

I won't allow her to.

I wind several lengths around her chest to secure her to the back of the chair then check her purse. I find nothing of interest. I examine her phone, since she brought it with her downstairs, checking texts or recent calls, but there aren't any at all. Almost like the history has been cleared. Then again, maybe she just brought the phone to use the flashlight function.

What was she up to at my desk?

I get an ice pack from the freezer for her head. I wrap it in a towel and bring it to her.

Of course, now I have to hold it because her hands are tied. I place one foot on either side of her knee and press the ice against the puffy lump above her left eye. I use my other hand to catch the opposite side of her head to hold it in place. I tip her face up.

She glares at me from under her pale lashes.

"One twist and I could snap this pretty neck of yours."

She shifts her gaze to stare through my chest. "You won't." She has a stubborn, resolute look.

Blyad.'

She already knows I'm too soft to hurt her.

"What makes you so sure?" I make my tone gruff. Menacing.

Normally, I frighten women and men alike. I'm big, covered in tattoos, and look like I could eat their mothers for breakfast.

Her gaze jogs left and returns. "The ice pack was a big clue."

Right. I tipped my hand there, didn't I?

I give her what I hope is an alarming smile. "That doesn't mean I don't want to hurt you."

She stiffens and strains against her bonds, but her nipples bead up under the t-shirt.

"There are many forms of torture, little warrior. I'll find ones suited to such a pretty package." I stroke my thumb down her cheek, then remove the ice and leave her.

I keep the light on in the living room, walk to my bedroom, and for the second time tonight, take off my clothes and climb under the covers.

Kira can simmer there in her chair in a lit room for the

rest of the night. We'll see what a little sleep deprivation does to get my little Valkyrie to talk.

If that doesn't work, I will have to figure out other ways to make her sing.

* * *

Sleep deprivation.

Good start, but it won't work. I learned to control my mind years ago. I had to crawl out of the hole I was born into. To make something of myself after the bratva killed my father and ruined my sister.

I close my eyes and focus on my breath. Tell myself to fall into a deep and restorative sleep. Sink deeper with each exhale. I tell myself I will awake feeling refreshed and renewed, knowing exactly how to escape.

My eyes flicker back open. Maykl stands in front of me, staring down with a troubled frown on his face.

I don't know what time it is, but I know I've been through at least one sleep cycle, maybe two. It's not morning yet–no light shines through the blinds on his large windows.

Maykl kneels in front of me and cuts loose the wrap on my ankles and then my chest. He closes his meaty hand around my upper arm and hauls me to my feet.

I wince and stumble as the blood returns to my feet. Maykl grabs the roll of duct tape and maneuvers me into his bedroom. He leaves the light off.

"Get in the bed."

Somehow, I don't think he's ordering me to his bed for sex. That would be the logical conclusion, but he doesn't have that sexual edge to him right now that he had earlier. Like when he spanked me and slid his fingers between my legs.

The Gatekeeper

If he is interested in sex, I'm not sure what I would do.

Whether I should fight and show him I don't want it or return to my seduction of the enemy play.

I don't know whether I'm afraid of Maykl forcing sex on me or excited by it.

If I base my determination on our last encounter, I'm excited. But what he showed me last time is that he enjoys a little violence with sex. And if that was how he acted *before* he discovered I'm the enemy, how much rougher would he be? What would he demand of me?

I crawl in the bed, and he rolls me to my side and tapes my ankles together. He winds something soft and silky–must be the tie he used on my wrists yesterday when our sex was playful–and ties it snugly around my neck. It's not tight enough to choke me but enough that there's pressure there. Then he lies down behind me.

The tie around my neck tugs as he picks up the ends of it and wraps them around his fist.

"Try to get away this time, *Valkiriya*, and you'll find out how willing I am to snap your neck."

The corners of my lips tick up as I realize what just happened.

Oh, Maykl. Such empty threats. I smile to myself in the darkness.

He wasn't even willing to leave me to sleep in a chair all night. This guy may look like a monster–and I'm sure is a monster on many levels–but he's a fool when it comes to women.

Or when it comes to me.

I quash that thought as soon as it rises.

Of course, there's nothing special about me.

These bratva men like to keep women as objects. As toys or playthings. That's what Anya was to Aleksi, the man she came to Chicago with. He's dead now, too. Died in a shoot-out with the rest of his cell. What happened to Anya and Mika after that, I don't know.

For the years after the bratva exacted our father's payment from her, Anya sold herself to them. Found the man who would pay the most. Who would support her and Mika? Someone who didn't mind her drug addiction. Didn't need her to be anything but willing.

The bratva aren't permitted to marry. It's part of the code. That's why sex is always transactional with them.

I attempt to roll a bit forward to alleviate the pain in my shoulders from having my hands bound behind my back for so long, but it tugs on the choker around my neck.

I shove backward to make it possible, my ass hitting Maykl's loins. His dick surges between my legs.

Oh, boy.

I'm less afraid now, though. More sure that this man can be manipulated or maneuvered or somehow tricked into letting me go by his unwillingness to harm me.

I test my theory. "Please. My arms are killing me. I can't lie in this position, Maykl."

He doesn't move or speak, but I suspect he's thinking it over.

"Please? Just a change of position. Tie them in front of me. Or over my head. My shoulders hurt."

"You're a prisoner. Pain is to be expected." His voice is gruff, but I imagine I hear the notes of him convincing himself.

I try to think of a good answer to that but can't come up with one.

After a few moments of charged silence, Maykl grunts and gets up. When he returns, I feel the blade of his scissors before they snip through the tape. I groan as the blood rushes down my arms, needles and pins prickling everywhere. I open and close my fingers and shake my elbows to speed the process.

"Thank you," I murmur. "Thank you so much." I might as well give him a bit of sugar. That's certainly the right measure with a man like him.

He rolls me to my other side and tapes not just my wrists together, but my fingers and thumbs, as well–no doubt so I can't use them to free myself. When he finishes, he wraps his fist in the ends of the tie once more and pulls me toward him, so my face is right in front of his.

"Be good, *moya malen'kaya Valkiriya*, or I'll make you suffer."

Lies, I suspect.

"Thank you," I whisper again.

In the darkness, I see his frown. He knows I'm playing him again.

I know he's letting me.

It's an uneasy truce, but it definitely could be worse.

Far, far worse.

Chapter Seven

Maykl

I rise with the sun and get up to shower. I liked having my little warrior settled beside me far more than I liked her out in the living room where I couldn't see her. Where I was worried about her discomfort.

Blyad'. I don't know how I'm going to get any information out of her when I'm so unwilling to inflict even the smallest amount of pain.

I make my shower quick and discover my sense of urgency was correct. She's rolled herself off the bed and is crawling her way across the floor like an inchworm.

Considering the state of her undress, it's a very alluring sight. I watch her, letting her keep it up as I pull my clothes out and get dressed. Letting her entertain me with her bare ass undulating to the sky like she's humping my floor.

"That's pretty, *malen'kaya Valkiriya*."

She knew I was in the room. I'm sure she knew the moment the shower stopped that I'd find her. She sighs and rolls over onto her back to look at me. "I have to pee."

I love that she's not afraid of me. That she's making petulant demands.

That's wrong.

I should definitely want her to be afraid. How else will I get the information I need from her?

But it satisfies me on some deep level that she's not traumatized by what I've put her through. That she still has her indomitable warrior spirit and is fighting back in the ways she can.

I give her a glimmer of a smile and tilt my head toward the bathroom. "Then you're going in the wrong direction."

She holds her bound hands out like she wants me to help her up.

I shake my head and fold my arms across my chest. "*Nyet*. I am enjoying the show. *Thoroughly*. Please continue, little warrior. It's a lovely sight."

She huffs her displeasure but manages to roll back to her belly and make a 180 to start inching in my direction.

Fuck.

So. Hot.

I never thought I'd be the type of guy who fantasized about keeping a woman captive. Forcing her to crawl. To serve.

But everything about this scenario is turning me on.

Until I notice the rug burn on her forearms.

I lurch forward and scoop her up to balance on her bound legs then toss her over my shoulder to carry to the bathroom. I let my hand slide up the back of her bare thigh.

She smells like sugar cookies and warm bread and faintly of sex.

I set her down in front of the toilet and stand over her as she lowers to sit on the seat, pinning me with a defiant look.

Showing me she's not cowed by my handling or intimidated by me towering over her, watching as she uses the toilet.

She makes a show of using the blade of her taped hands to unroll a length of toilet paper then raises her brows at me expectantly.

I waffle between telling her to drip-dry and helping. Which is more disempowering?

Since I don't intend to allow her to dress, I decide helping is the best option. I finish and inspect her elbows and knees. The skin is chafed. She'll probably get little scabs, but there's no real harm.

Still, I don't like seeing any kind of marks on her.

Except my handprint on her ass.

I like that. A lot.

I carry her back to the bed and toss her on it, climbing over to snip off the tape around her wrists and pull her arms behind her back again. "You shouldn't have tried to run away, *Valkiriya*. Now I have to punish you."

She turns her head, trying to gaze at me over her shoulder. Her bare ass is tempting me to do all kinds of dirty things to her. I lean over and bite one cheek, hard.

But she's not my plaything.

I need to interrogate her today. Find out what she's doing here. Who sent her. What her objective was in searching my desk. Is it related to her sister's death? Her search for her nephew? Does she still believe he's here?

My shift begins at noon, so I need to get answers soon.

I scoop her delectable body into my arms and carry her back to the living room, where I tape her back in the chair. Once more, having her tied to my kitchen chair pleases me. It inspires an affection toward her rather than animosity. I don't want to harm her, but I also don't want to give her her freedom back.

Ever.

I ruffle her silky hair before I walk away.

In the kitchen, I scramble a pan of eggs and put toast in the toaster. I make enough for her to eat, too, even though I know the logical thing would be for me to refuse to feed her. To eat in front of her as a torment and wait until she grows hungry and desperate enough to talk.

If I'm not willing to spill her blood or bruise her body, it's a fairly benign way to go.

Still, I can't make myself do it.

I'm cocking this thing up. Big time.

I cocked up letting her into the building, and now I'm making things worse. I'm the head of security at the Kremlin, and I've allowed this slip of a woman to plow over me to get into the building.

Especially because I already decided I'm not going to Ravil.

I can't let them torture her. I know the kinds of things they're capable of. I've been there. Witnessed what happens down in the basement where blood can be washed down a drain and concrete floors can be bleached.

So I pile a plate high with the food, and I carry it over. I stand in front of her and assemble a piece of buttered toast with a heap of scrambled egg on top. Take a large bite and chew it slowly.

She watches me.

I turn the piece of toast around to face her and offer her a bite.

Her bite isn't dainty. She almost bites off as much as I did and chews quickly.

I chuckle. "You were hungry."

"Being tied up burns a lot of calories."

I grin. "Get used to it, *Valkiriya*. I like having you tied to my chair. I might not ever let you go."

I take another bite of toast. "Why were you searching my desk? What did you hope to find?"

"I was looking for a pen."

She's full of sass this morning.

I try to think from her perspective. What would she think a doorman had?

"You wanted a list of the occupants of the building."

I can tell I'm right by the way something closes off behind her eyes. Like she put up a shield.

"Who are you after? My *pakhan?*"

It occurs to me I haven't searched her suitcase yet. I give her another bite of toast then open her suitcase on the coffee table in the living room and take every item out. There's nothing in it. Clothing. A few cosmetics. I search the lining of the bag for a hidden compartment.

Nothing.

I find her purse and search it again. This time, I notice the lining is ripped by the handle. No–not ripped.

It's been neatly cut. I sweep my hand along the bag, feeling for what might be under the lining and touch some kind of card.

I yank the lining out of the purse and pull out the object.

It's an ID card.

"You're Russian police."

Her chin lifts, a stubborn set to her jaw.

I consider the implications. She can't be here on official business. The bratva owns the police in Moscow. Besides, if she were here in an official capacity, she wouldn't have come alone. She would have a partner. But it explains why she seemed trained to fight. She's a complicated mix of transparency and intrigue, vulnerability and edge. She's hiding something, and all of our lives may hinge on it. On me figuring it out.

I read her name again. *Koslova.*

Cold ice washes over me. No. Koslova is a common name.

It's a coincidence.

My mouth has gone dry. I pick up my phone and text Dima. He lives a few hours away in the small town where his girlfriend Natasha is studying to become a naturopath. He might do this favor for me without alerting Ravil.

I need a favor, I text. *Could you get me any information you pull on Kira Koslova? She's Russian police, from Moscow.* I enter her passport ID. *Specifically, I'd like the names of her parents and what division of* politsiya *she works in.*

Dima texts back immediately. *Give me a few hours.*

Thank you. Also, could we keep this between the two of us for now?

He texts back with a thumb's up emoji.

I saunter back to her side, my mind spinning. I offer her another bite of toast as I consider her. "You're here on some vendetta."

I catch the surprise in her expression before she suppresses it and know I guessed correctly.

Blyad.'

Could she be related to the man I killed all those years ago? The murder required to admit me as a full member of the bratva?

Does she know I'm the one who pulled the trigger? Is she here to kill me?

The thought sobers me.

I've lived with the weight of that murder for more than

half my life. For some reason, it haunts me far more than killing my own father.

I scrub a hand across my face to erase the images that rise to my mind. His pleading eyes. The stench of fear.

I feed the rest of the toast to Kira, my own appetite suddenly lost.

I should let her go. If she craves revenge, I'm willing to give her a shot at it.

But no. She would have killed me in my sleep the first night. Unless she's not sure it was me.

No...she either doesn't know who killed him, or she's really here for the nephew, or she just wants revenge for her sister.

Or perhaps some other reason. Or all of them. I need to find out.

I must do my job as gatekeeper and protect my cell.

Chapter Eight

K*ira*
Light filters in through the blinds. Maykl walks over and cracks them, revealing a breathtaking view of Lake Michigan. It's bigger than I imagined, stretching as far as the eye can see–like an ocean. The water is grey-blue to match the winter sky.

He has an entire wall of windows. As he walks the length of it and cracks each of the blinds, it's like he's changing the distorted pictures in my mind.

What I expected to find of the Chicago bratva vs. what is actually here.

In Moscow, the bratva lived together, like here. They had a more clandestine location. An old pre-war brick hospital that had been converted to house them. They must have had money, but it wasn't fancy, like this building. It wasn't showy.

I remember going in looking for Anya once, and it had more of a crack house feel to it than a residence. Not disgusting like the place Anya lived in here, but underground.

There were random people drinking and doing drugs. Dancing. Having sex. Everyone was heavily armed and menacing.

There was a distinctly dangerous edge to the scene. It represented the seedy underbelly of Moscow. A place where teenage girls were taken to work off their father's debts.

This place–at least Maykl's apartment–seems like an ordinary residence. If ordinary means luxurious with a priceless view. The front lobby looked like the lobby of any luxury high-rise, with the exception of the heavily armed and tattooed doorman.

I'm not fooled–I know they're criminals. Perhaps far more dangerous than the cell in Moscow. Certainly better funded and organized.

But the beauty makes it harder to judge. So does Maykl's kindness. His sexiness.

It's almost harder not to spill my guts to him than it would be if he was beating me and ripping off fingernails.

I know this is a different technique used with captives. Bond them to their captors. Somehow gain their allegiance and trust.

I have to be careful.

Everything's so mixed up and jumbled for me because we were intimate. Because he helped me with Anya's funeral arrangements.

The way he ruffled my hair after securing me to the chair did strange things to my mind.

It made me almost *crave* his attention. His approbation.

He ignores me for a while, washing the breakfast dishes, cleaning up. When he returns, he lifts a water glass to my lips and lets me drink from it.

I swallow several gulps down.

I want to interrogate *him* now. Find out what goes on in this building. If I'd been smart, I would have taken more time to cultivate something with him. Win his trust.

But I don't have the time or the money to play a long game here. And I was blinded by my desperation and grief at finding Mika missing.

I guess my own anger with myself for not coming sooner–the moment I lost contact with Anya–made my behavior erratic.

Maykl faces me, leaning against the edge of his desk to consider me. He doesn't seem angry. Nor does he seem turned on, like before. I sense something more like sympathy from him. He strokes my cheek softly with his large thumb.

"Who are you avenging, *Valkiriya*?" he asks softly. "Anya?"

The question takes me aback. That he would guess so astutely why I'm here. What I want.

I shake my head. "I'm looking for Mika," I assert because it's true, and sticking to the truth is my best bet.

"You think I lied? That we really have him?" He shakes his head. "There's no one with the name Koslova here." He raises his brows. "Did you think we had something to do with Anya? With her death?"

I continue to remain close-lipped.

"We've bought Russian sex slaves, yes, but to set them free. Some have remained as a choice. No women are imprisoned here, I promise you that, Kira."

They bought Russian sex slaves. That statement shocks my nervous system. The way he says it so casually. Like human trafficking is something they see every day. Are a part of.

But, of course, he claimed they aren't.

I attempt to digest the information without showing any reaction. They set them free *after* they used them? Like they took my sister to pay off our father's debt?

Or did they buy them for the purpose of setting them free?

I chew it over, not sure what to believe. My past and everything I know about the bratva in Moscow tells me these men do as they please. If it makes them feel magnanimous to free slaves they never should have owned in the first place, they'll do that.

They do have certain codes they follow.

Maykl stands over me, his beefy arms folded across his chest. "I have a hundred ways of making you talk, *Valkiriya*. Believe it."

I give him a sullen stare.

"I don't want to spill your blood or mar your pretty face. That doesn't mean I won't find other ways."

I avert my face, purposely looking to the lovely view.

Maykl grips my jaw and turns my face to his. "Why are you really here?"

I remain silent.

Maykl's lips thin. He releases my jaw and moves behind me. I watch his reflection in the window to see him retrieve his gun–from the freezer of all places–and walk out the door.

In the silence that stretches after leaves, I'm both relieved and worried.

Did he go to get his bratva brothers? What is his plan with me? When will he be back?

Actually, none of that matters. He left me alone. Now I just need to figure out my way out of this chair, so I can call Stepanov and escape the building.

The Gatekeeper

* * *

Maykl

I let Kira stew. I need to go downstairs and relieve Gleb of his duties at the front desk. Besides, I need to figure out the best way to proceed, and the longer I stay, the more I show my hand to her.

Truth serum. That's what I need. In the 1980's, the KGB pioneered a soluble drug–SP-117– that was odorless, colorless and tasteless. It causes the recipient to lose control fifteen minutes after intake.

Maxim has some. He's our fixer. He's used the drug to strategic ends in the past. The problem is, if I ask him for it, he's going to wonder why I need it.

Obviously, I should go to him and Ravil. Explain everything, including my solution, which is to use the drug on Kira to find out exactly who she works for and what she's after.

I pull my phone out of my pocket and look at the screen, my thumb hovering over it without touching it.

Blyad.'

What if she's working for one of our enemies?

They could be after Sasha, Maxim's wife, hoping to kill or capture her to get at that fortune. The interest in those wells gives Ravil a stronghold inside the Russian government. This is how he smuggles his goods from Russia to America without hindrance. Those who control the oil, control government officials around the world. Every other branch of bratva is after what Ravil now has. That's the power grab and part of what makes our cell so powerful and dangerous.

Kira could certainly be a part of that ploy.

Sending a beautiful Russian woman pretending to need refuge is an excellent way to get someone into the building.

A tight coil of danger winds around my trunk.

I let her in here. I could be the weak link that brings about our demise. If that were true, I could never live with myself.

I swipe across my screen and dial Maxim's number.

"Maykl."

Fuck. I hesitate.

Why am I so damn unwilling to turn Kira over to them? What is this hold she seems to have over me?

"Maykl?" he repeats.

"Yes, Maxim. Listen..." I think quickly. "Do you know where I can get my hands on a couple doses of SP-117?" I speak in English because that's what Ravil requires of us when we speak to each other. He wants us to master the language, so we can move seamlessly through this country.

"Why?"

I knew he'd ask me. I should have prepared a story.

Instead, I growl, "It's a private matter."

Silence.

Then Maxim says, "Okay," with a surprised lilt. "I'll bring some down."

Relief sweeps through me. "Thank you."

I sit behind the desk and tap a pen against the counter, pulling up the camera I set up on Kira.

She appears to be struggling against her bonds.

She won't get free. I used enough duct tape to keep a small car from moving. It reminds me to grab some zip ties from the desk drawer, though. They might be easier than tape in some instances.

Like in the shower.

That thought gets my dick hard. Remembering what

Kira looked like that first night, walking naked out of my bathroom, toweling off her silky blonde hair.

If she's my prisoner for long, she'll need another shower. And, of course, I won't be able to trust her in there by herself. I'll have to assist.

Soap those lovely soft curves. Slip my fingers into all her nooks and crannies. Make sure she's squeaky clean before I put her in my bed again.

Maxim arrives off the elevator, his hands casually stuffed in his pockets. He walks to the front desk and pulls out a small blister pack containing six pills–three red, three white.

"It works in fifteen minutes. Dissolve the white one in any liquid, but alcohol is best if you don't want them to know something happened. The victim will just think he's groggy from the liquor."

I nod.

Maxim points to the red pills. "Give them a dose of the red when you're finished, and they'll come out of it without knowing anything happened. They won't remember telling you anything. If you don't care, the second pill isn't necessary." He gives me a scrutinizing look.

I keep my face blank and nod. "Thank you."

"Personal matter, huh?"

I eye him. He's very much my superior. Our *pakhan's* right-hand man. He certainly could compel me to talk. Still, I remain resolute. "That's right."

He shrugs. "I see. Well, I'm here if you need a strategist."

I suck in a breath. "*Da.* Thanks. Thank you. I appreciate that."

Maxim nods, still thoughtful. He hesitates a moment

like he's going to say something more, then turns and strides back to the elevator.

I wait until I hear the doors close before I relax back into my chair and open my palm to examine the pills.

Not telling him was the right solution.

I let Kira in here, it's on me to find out what she's up to. If I discover anything, I'll notify my bratva brothers then.

I already know that decision will probably bite me in the ass, but I hate the alternative. Kira's my problem to deal with. No one else touches her if I can do anything about it.

* * *

Kira

No amount of twisting and turning my hands has loosened the duct tape around them. Nor can I bust my ankles free from the chair legs.

The best option may be to try to break the chair.

I throw my body to the side, encouraging the chair to tip up onto two legs.

It drops back into place.

I rock again and again. Sometimes, I succeed only in making the chair slide instead of tip. Eventually, though, I get it to tilt enough that it falls.

What I didn't count on, was my weight carrying it backward at the same time.

My head smacks something hard before I even hit the ground, and everything goes black.

I blink my eyes open.

Gospodi, it's too bright in here.

My head splinters with pain.

I let out a whimper.

"That was unwise, little warrior. What were you thinking?"

Only then do I realize Maykl is here with me, working quickly to cut me free. My arms burst into an explosion of pain as they are released from their position behind my back.

Maykl holds my face and turns it, examining me with his brows down. "Look at me, Kira," he murmurs in Russian.

I meet his gaze. He studies my eyes, no doubt looking for pupils that are different sizes. Signs of a concussion. I did take a pretty hard knock to the head. I must've been out for more than a few seconds if he had time to get up here although he does seem slightly out of breath like he ran up the stairs rather than wait for the elevator.

I groan.

"Very unwise. You hit your head on the desk and then again on the floor."

Realizing my hands are free and he's focused on my injuries, I trail my fingers along the waistband of his jeans, searching for the pistol.

It's not there.

He catches my wrist, brings my hand to his mouth, and bites the meaty part of my thumb.

My pussy clenches, and I squeak, more in surprise than in pain although it does hurt. What kind of man bites his captive as punishment? The same kind who spanks her instead of cutting her thumbs off, I suppose.

I try to ignore the flutters this man ignites in me.

I don't need to get distracted by the physical attraction between us. By the gentle way he handles me as he frees my ankles and lifts me off the chair.

My brain tells me to fight, that this is my moment, my

hands and legs are free. I should do as much damage as I can and get myself out of here.

But, for some reason, I hesitate. Maybe it's the fact that my arms are still on fire with pins and needles. Or because I haven't found what I came here for, yet.

It can't be because this man is affecting me. That I enjoy the way he's running his hands over my body, checking for other injuries with a flare of concern. That I don't want to harm him because he hasn't harmed me.

And it's true that considering our size and weight differences, I'd have to aim to hurt him badly if I wanted to escape. He's a beast of a man and built of solid muscle. Taking him down would have to involve a major trauma to the head or deadly force. Even if I managed to get his gun, I suspect he could disarm me.

I've never shot a man. I'm trained, yes, and I've drawn a weapon before, but I've never been the one to pull the trigger.

"I need to use the bathroom," I announce.

"Go." He jerks his head toward the bedroom.

I'm surprised he's willing to let me go on my own. I'd be stupid not to use the time to my advantage. I move on wobbly legs, my head throbbing where I hit it. I use the toilet and wash up, then scan the room for weapons. I choose the easiest one–the toilet tank lid. It's heavy and ceramic. If I use it to smash Maykl's head, it will give me a chance to get away.

But it's too late. The bathroom door swings open.

I haul the toilet cover back to swing, but he knocks it out of my hands before I get the change. He's fast for such a big man.

He spins me around, securing me in a chokehold against his body.

"Still fighting, little warrior?" His voice is a purr in my ear. A rich, amused rumble, like he finds it adorable that I want to fight him. That I'm trying to free myself. "You're earning yourself one hell of a punishment."

That makes the flesh between my legs contract and squeeze. My belly flutters.

I have to face the fact that my hesitation–my reluctance to fight my way out of here–is what cost me the few precious seconds I lacked to launch my attack. I may be as ambivalent about Maykl as he is about me.

He bites my ear, hard enough to make me squirm. Heat floods my nether region. My nipples harden against his thin t-shirt. He eases his forearm away from my windpipe and allows his hand to settle over my breast, squeezing roughly.

Another bite to my shoulder.

This guy likes to use his teeth. I shouldn't find that sexy.

It's not sexy at all.

It's...

Damn. Okay, it is hot. I never thought such a thing would turn me on, but it does.

He keeps one arm wrapped tightly around my waist but uses his other hand to whip the t-shirt off me. "You lost your clothing privileges," he growls.

My heart patters against my chest. For some reason, I can't come up with a single response. No words. No fight. My brain stalls completely.

"I'll get cold," I complain. It's a weak argument against his dictate.

"I'll turn up the heat."

He folds my hands up behind my neck, which has the effect of lifting and separating my breasts.

"I...you..."

Seriously–why can't I think of anything to say at all? I

don't usually turn into the deer in the headlights. Maykl rotates me slowly to face him. His gaze is dark, lids at half-mast as he takes in my naked form.

"I am thinking of many terrible things to do to you." The low, growly threat makes it sound far more like he's planning pleasure than pain.

Pleasure for himself, perhaps.

Arousal soaks my sex, as if preparing me for that sort of assault.

He turns me toward the door and walks me out. "Lie face down on the bed." He releases me.

I bolt for the door. I'm completely naked and without any weapon, but if he thinks I'm going to go put myself in position for his punishment, he's nuts.

I make it three steps before he catches me by the throat. He lifts me from my feet, cutting off my breath.

"One snap of this delicate neck would end your life," he warns.

I know it's a bluff because he sets me back on my feet and restores my breath before I even see stars.

"You're testing my patience, *Valkiriya*." In a series of swift moments, he pins my hands back behind my back–the position that makes my arms scream–and secures my wrists with a plastic zip tie. "I like to wrestle with you, but I desire a little more cooperation."

"We don't always get what we desire, do we?" I snark.

"Ah, but this time, I think I will."

I ponder those words as he propels me back to the chair. I dig my heels in. "No."

The thought of returning to that particular prison makes me balk, but he pushes me back down and tapes my thighs down to the seat.

"You see? You could be lying in a soft bed right now. Instead, you chose to make things hard."

I grit my teeth and glare, but he disappears from my sight. I hear him in the kitchen and when he returns, he brings more ice for my head and a glass of water that he presses to my lips. I drink deeply, thirsty from going all morning without anything to drink.

Maykl stands and holds the ice pack to the new bruise on my head. He doesn't attempt conversation. He doesn't seem angry or vengeful. Simply watchful.

It's not until my eyelids start to droop and a deep relaxation washes over my limbs that I realize I've been drugged.

Chapter Nine

Maykl

My little warrior, fighting at every turn.

I watched her knock herself out tipping the chair over and nearly broke a leg sprinting up the steps to get to her. Thank God, she doesn't seem too badly injured.

I'll have to think of some other solution for keeping her prisoner. Something relatively comfortable but secure.

The fact that she's naked now is doing screwy thing to my brain, though. I cut her free from the chair. I'm going to have to get a new roll of duct tape if I keep this up much longer. I throw her over my shoulder to carry my Valkyrie into the bedroom and lay her on the bed. She's awake but clearly drugged. Her body is limp, her gaze unfocused and glassy.

"What did you give me?" she mumbles.

"Truth serum." I cut her wrists free and rearrange her into a comfortable position on her side. I forgot to turn my heat up, so I pull the covers around her now and then sit beside her, brushing the cornsilk of her hair from her face.

"What is your name?"

"You already know it," she mutters. "I'm Kira Koslova."

Who sent you, Kira? The *politsiya*?"

Her brows knit. "I sent myself," she mumbles.

"Why?"

She appears to be fighting the drug. She rolls her head to one side and the other.

I stroke her cheek. "Shh. Relax. The truth will set us all free, Kira Koslova. Why are you here?"

"To find my nephew."

"What were you looking for in the desk?"

"Information."

"Why not ask?"

"I...don't...trust bratva."

As I suspected. "What do you know about the bratva?"

She shakes her head. "Hate...bratva."

"Because of Anya?"

"Yes. And the brava killed my father."

I barely keep the groan from my lips. This revelation physically pains me. All these years I've been haunted by my actions. That I executed a man without knowing a thing about him. That he had two daughters.

I was thirteen years old, and they told me to shoot. I did as I was told. It's no excuse. There's no forgiveness. Ravil has said we wear the tattoos on our skin as reminders of our sin.

That we are not clean. We are marked by the violence, blood, and death that has been wrought in the name of the bratva.

He does not seem to relish the markings on his skin like most bratva leaders. It's more like a weight he requires himself to carry. I've appreciated his take on it because killing never came easily to me.

The Gatekeeper

I don't sleep at night without being haunted by the faces of the men I've ended.

Particularly my first–Grigor Koslov.

Somehow, though, I manage not to show anything to Kira.

"Who killed your father?" I ask. She didn't accuse me of the execution. But did she come here looking for me?

"I told you: bratva. He owed them money. First, they took my sister. They made her work off his debt and left her pregnant with Mika. Then he angered them again. I don't know how. All I know is that of our two parents, he was the one who cared, and the bratva took him."

I manage to keep my breath steady and even, though inside a restless wind has whipped into a frenzy.

I killed this beautiful woman's father. Left her orphaned. With a sister impregnated by men from my cell.

I don't remember her sister–it must have been before my initiation.

Of course, her father had offered Anya's body up as payment. He'd offered Kira's, too. So, I guess considering that I'm almost glad the bratva didn't accept his offer. I would hate for Kira to have suffered the same way her sister did. Still, she lost a parent at my hands.

"I'm sorry."

"My sister never recovered. She became an addict. I helped raise my nephew, but she took him with her when she moved to America with her bratva boyfriend."

"Who was her boyfriend?"

"Aleksi."

"There is no Aleksi here. You have the wrong cell–I told you that before. You didn't believe me?"

"He's dead. Now, so is Anya." Kira flops a hand across

her eyes and her lips tremble. "It's my fault. I should have come to find him sooner."

My chest aches with her pain. I want to take it away. To hunt this boy down for her. Unbreak her heart.

"Kira." I lift the hand away from her eyes. "He's not here. I wasn't lying."

She shakes her head. "I don't trust bratva."

That coil of sickness in my gut winds tighter. She's right not to trust me. I am the man who murdered her father.

Her blue eyes swim with tears. "I lost him," she moans.

I brush one of the tears sliding down her temple away. "Maybe we can find him. I will help you, *Valkiriya*."

"Why are you so kind to me?"

I ignore her question. "What were you doing breaking into my desk?"

"Looking for information–the list of who lives here. A building diagram."

"Why?"

Her eyes droop closed, then open. "I came in grief. Directly from the morgue and a visit to the crack house where my sister lived. They told me there was no boy with her and hadn't been for several years. So, I came in hope and dread that Mika had attached himself to the bratva to survive. The police officer told me you take in Russians."

Ah. So, this was who she meant when she said she was told we would help.

The story is coming together.

"Who are you working with?"

She shakes her head, pressing her lips closed. A soft moan issues from behind them.

"Who, Kira?"

"The..." she appears to be fighting the drug. "FBI."

I go still. Fuck.

"What do they want?"

"They wanted me to plant bugs and..." Again, she seems to be trying to stop herself from speaking.

"And what, Kira?"

"I sent the code to the front door."

"What else?"

"Photos of the lobby and stairwell. Also of the HVAC system."

"Where did you plant the bugs?"

"In both elevators and the pottery studio. Under your desk. I'm supposed to put one in your *pakhan's* office."

I scrub a hand over my face. Thank fuck Ravil didn't have time to see her yesterday. I will have to tell him, though. And soon.

"Who is your contact with the FBI?"

She shakes her head. "My boss has the contact. He said if I helped them get into the Kremlin, they would help me find Mika."

"The name of your boss?"

"Stepanov. Anton Stepanov."

"The name of his FBI contact?"

Again, she shakes her head. "I don't know. Stepanov won't tell me."

A knock sounds on my door.

Blyad'.

I throw a blanket over Kira's naked form, quickly replace the zip ties on her wrists and ankles and go to answer it.

As if things weren't already bad enough with Kira bugging the building and working with the FBI, when the door swings open, I find my *pakhan*.

Which means I'm fucked, and so is Kira.

Chapter Ten

Maykl

Ravil has a deceiving manner of appearing laid-back. Casual. As if he couldn't order your murder with a wave of his finger.

Now, his hands are tucked in the pockets of his designer slacks, his button-down is open at the throat. Behind him stand Maxim and Nikolai.

I make an attempt to appear equally casual. "What can I do for you, *Pakhan*?"

Ravil blinks once. Twice. The silence is excruciating. Then he says, "You can tell me what's going on with the woman in your apartment."

I attempt to swallow and fail.

There's nothing that can be done. No way I can keep any of this from him. Kira is working with the FBI. My boss may kill her. Her fate is out of my hands now.

I go for brief and direct. "I allowed her to enter the building the night before last. She came to Chicago to claim her dead sister's body and find her nephew. That much is true. But what I didn't know until recently is that she is *politsiya* working with the FBI in exchange for information about her nephew."

Ravil tips his head to look past me. "Where is she now?"

"Zip tied to my bed."

Nikolai's brows flick ever-so-slightly. Maxim's lips twitch.

But Ravil is unamused. "When were you going to tell me about this situation?"

Heat prickles up the back of my neck.

In the bratva, betraying a brother is cause for death. In my experience, this rule can be invoked for the slightest transgression. Many things can and have been construed as betrayals.

Certainly, my allowing Kira to infiltrate and bug our building could be seen as more than a failure to do my duty. It could be seen as a betrayal of my brothers.

I steel my chest like a soldier in the military rather than a crime organization. "Immediately. I've been interrogating her this afternoon."

Ravil raises his brows as if he doesn't believe me.

I absorb the gaze without flinching. Showing him I am still loyal, despite my fuck-up.

"She's secure? Can you leave her?"

I nod.

"Come to my office."

"Get her phone or any electronics she brought with her," Nikolai says.

They wait for me as I get her purse and phone.

In the elevator, I put my fingers to my lips, searching for the bug. I find it behind the handrail. A tiny green light indicates it's on.

I hand it to Nikolai, who inspects it, then turns it off.

Maxim rummages through her purse. Nikolai takes the

phone and discovers a handful more bugs in the sleeve on her case. I was an idiot not to find them.

Blyad'. Does that mean the FBI overheard the entire conversation I just had with Kira?

But no, the bugs in her phone are not lit with the same green light. They haven't been turned on.

Maxim inspects Kira's *politsiya* badge and her passport.

"You used the truth serum on her?" Maxim asks.

I nod. "I couldn't bring myself to torture her. She is..." What? Heartbreakingly beautiful? Has me wrapped around her finger? "A small thing," I finish lamely.

Nikolai rolls his eyes. "You mean you fucked her, and now you can't stop thinking with your dick."

I bristle, but Nikolai is my superior. I can't tell him to fuck off, much as I'd like to.

"Did you?" Ravil asks in that mild manner of his.

I grit my teeth and nod.

When we get to the top floor, Ravil points at the bug in Nikolai's hand. "Turn it back on and leave it in the hallway. If they don't know we've found them yet, I'd like to keep it that way."

Nikolai does so, placing it above the doorway to the penthouse.

Inside, I hear Sasha's voice from a bedroom, as if she's talking on the phone.

The nanny plays with Benjamin on the carpet.

We all follow Ravil to his spacious office and pull up chairs. Nikolai opens a laptop, and his twin, Dima joins the conference via video feed.

Ravil steeples his fingers together. "Tell me."

I give the entire story, beginning with Kira showing up after closing time and ending with everything I just learned from my interrogation, excluding the fact that I executed her father.

"Plug her phone in to upload the contents," Dima requests, and Nikolai, seeming to understand what his twin needs, plugs the phone in and activates some kind of program.

Ravil opens his phone and makes a call.

"Alex?" Ravil addresses our insider at the FBI. A young man who shot Nikolai and wanted to kill Ravil last year because he believed Ravil had killed his father. It turned out to be a misunderstanding. Ravil spared his life and now owns the young man.

"I have a Russian policewoman here, Kira Koslova. She says she's working with the FBI. She planted bugs in my building."

Ravil listens for a while, staring at me the entire time. I'm sweating, but I remain as stoic as I know how under his gaze. When he ends the call he says, "There's no warrant, nor is there documentation about Kira being an asset."

"She could be a pocket asset," Nikolai says, referring to spies who are kept out of the system for various reasons.

The clack and clatter of Dima's keys comes through the video feed. "Everything Maykl reports can be verified except the FBI involvement. I did find one very interesting piece of information, though."

"What's that?" Maxim asks.

"Her boss is a pocket asset."

"To the FBI?"

"No. Moscow bratva."

"Ah." Ravil sits back in his chair, relaxing as if this was good news, rather than bad. "So, Kuznets is coming after me now."

"Or after Sasha." Maxim appears murderous.

"So what do they have, exactly?" Ravil prompts.

"My security code and four bugs," I say.

"Hang on," Dima says. "I'm checking her sent messages. Looks like the recipient is in the same geolocation."

"Stepanov is here in Chicago?" Maxim asks.

"Yes," Dima says. "Stand by for her texts." The screen flashes and loads with a string of messages that didn't appear on Kira's phone when I looked.

They include photos of the lobby, elevators, and stairwell, as well as of the underground parking entrance and HVAC system.

"So. Kira's police boss told her if she becomes their insider here, the FBI will help her locate her missing nephew," Ravil says. He looks at me. "She doesn't know her boss is in the bratva's pocket?"

I shake my head. "I don't think so. She hates the bratva. And she cried over her missing nephew while on the truth serum. Her grief seemed real."

"Did you find anything about the nephew?" Nikolai asks his twin.

"I have an idea about the boy," Ravil says.

"What is it?" asks Maxim.

"Vladimir. His cell was wiped out by the Tacone crime Family, remember?" Ravil directs his words to Maxim. "He worked under Victor. A different branch of the brava."

Maxim nods. "Ah, yes. He ended up marrying into the Italian mafia in a strange turn of fate."

"Yes. He kidnapped their sister for revenge but then later claimed her. His cell must have been the one Anya and her son came over with, and I believe he has two adopted Russian children. Perhaps this boy is one of them. I'll make a call to find out."

Even though I'm in no position to ask questions or make demands, I have to ask. "What about Kira?" I ask.

Ravil considers. "When was the last call from her cell phone?" he asks Dima.

"Tuesday afternoon.

"So that was before you caught her in the lobby," Ravil says.

"Yes."

"Kuznets may not know she's been made. We can use that to our advantage."

"Absolutely," Maxim says. "We can lure them in and get them on our own turf."

"So, Maykl, you sit on Kira. We will use the bugs and her cell phone to draw them in." He tips his head at Nikolai. "Get him handcuffs and chains. I don't want her getting away."

Nikolai moves toward the door, but I don't get up. "What about...after? What happens to Kira?"

Ravil sharpens his voice, the first outward sign of his irritation with me. "I'll deal with her then."

Fuck.

"Yes, *Pakhan*." I bow my head.

"I'll deal with you then, too."

Double fuck. I suspected I wasn't off the hook for my failure to notify him the moment things went wrong.

"Yes, *Pakhan*." I get up and move toward the door.

"And Maykl," Ravil calls me back.

"Yes, *Pakhan*?"

"No more fuck-ups. No more lapses of judgment. She's your prisoner. If you let her go; if you let her make contact with anyone outside this building, I will cut your balls off to make sure you don't ever think with your dick again."

I grew up with this level of threat and intimidation, so it

shouldn't bother me. But because our leader is normally so mild and because he doesn't make idle threats, I register the threat viscerally.

I bow my head once more. "Forgive me, *Pakhan*."

He waves me away. "We will deal with apologies later. For now, I want your word you can handle your part. Or should we take control of the woman?"

"*No*." I practically snarl the word, even though my head is already on Ravil's chopping block.

Surprisingly, my *pakhan* appears more satisfied than angry with my tone. He sits back. "That's what I thought. Now go deal with her. I will put guards outside your door as backup."

Nikolai meets me in the elevator hallway with a pair of handcuffs and chains. He hands them to me but doesn't release them when I tug. "Listen, Maykl. When Ravil kidnapped Lucy and brought her here, Maxim told him there was only one option that would result in her not being a threat to the organization."

I stiffen, understanding that we're talking about whether Kira dies or not. "And what was that?"

"Make her fall in love." He releases his hold on the chains and flicks a brow. "So use those wisely." A slap on my shoulder, and he's gone, with me standing there in the hallway with a kick of lust running through me.

Winning Kira is the only way to save her life.

Game on.

* * *

Kira

I drift off to sleep after Maykl leaves.

When I wake, he's standing over me, a dark gleam in his

eye. My ankles and wrists have been cut loose. "What will I do with you, *Valkiriya?*"

It all comes back to me. The truth serum. The interrogation. What I told him.

Logically, I know I should be afraid. The fact that I'm not means the drug is still coursing through my veins. Keeping me sluggish and relaxed. In an open state. Still susceptible to any question he might ask.

"Don't kill me," I mumble in reply to his most likely rhetorical question.

His brows lower. It's hard to focus, but he appears troubled. Like killing me is on the table, but he won't enjoy it.

That means I may have some wiggle room if my brain and body ever come back online.

"It's not up to me now, little warrior. You involved the FBI. Planted bugs in our building and sent them the information they needed to breach the building. Why would they need that?"

"They believe you will resist arrest, and there will be a stand-off." I hear myself whimper without even knowing I was going to. "I don't want you killed, Maykl."

His expression softens. He crawls onto the bed, leaning over me. "Is that so?" He brushes my hair from my face.

"No. You'd be on the frontline. I don't like it. I was going to try to protect you."

His lips quirk. "Protect me." His deep growl of a voice warms my chest. "How would you protect me, *Valkiriya?*"

"I don't know. I would lure you away from the door. Or warn you. I didn't have a plan. I have been winging this whole thing if you couldn't tell."

It's strange to hear all my thoughts pour out of my mouth. So unlike me to share any personal thoughts at all.

I attempt to meet his gaze. My eyes still seem to have trouble focusing. "Would you try to protect me, Maykl?"

He stares down at me, conflict swirling behind his brown gaze.

"I know I don't deserve it. I lost your trust. But there's still something between us, isn't there?"

Gospodi. I sound pathetic. Why can't I wake from this dream-like state the drug put me in?

He grips my jaw, his stare hardening. "What is there between us, Kira, hmm? Sex?"

For a moment, I can't breathe. There's some emotion stuffed just behind my solar plexus.

Something fighting to get out.

My vision grows blurry. Am I crying over his rejection following my vulnerable attempt at finding common ground?

"You took pity on me before. You helped me with Anya's funeral arrangements."

"Yes and look how you repaid me."

I blink, and the tears spill down my temples into my ears. "I know. But it had to be done. To find Mika."

His expression only hardens further. His sympathy for me and my plight has ended.

"I'm sorry, Maykl."

It's true. We both know it's true because I'm still under the influence of the drug he gave me. Still unable to filter anything or lie.

That seems to soften him because he lowers his mouth to mine, still gripping my jaw. He devours me with a kiss, his tongue lashing between my lips, punishing me with the ferocity of the contact.

I kiss him back, still crying. Ecstatic at the touch. At the hope for redemption burning in my chest. It goes on and on.

A blinding kiss. The kind that makes my eyes roll back in my head and my mind go completely empty.

When he pulls away, I whimper at the loss.

"You like that, little warrior?" he murmurs.

"Yes," I moan. "I like... you. I–" I try to filter the words before they come out but fail. "I'm falling for you, but I don't want to."

One corner of his lips quirk. "That's cute, *Valkiriya*." He strokes his thumb along my lower lip. "I'm inclined to believe you."

"You have to believe me because you have me drugged," I moan.

He chuckles darkly.

"It's not funny."

He tucks his thumb in my mouth, and I suck on it, somehow eager to taste more of him. To please him.

"It's a little funny."

The idea of biting his thumb filters through my brain, but no part of me wants to take action on it.

"You are cute like this. I love to hear your unfiltered thoughts."

"What's going to happen to me?" I ask.

"I don't know." For some reason, I believe he is speaking the truth, too. "But for now, I am your prison guard. Which I like." His gaze turns feral. "Keeping you chained to my bed is a great pleasure."

I blink up at him. "What will you do with me...in your bed?" I don't think I'm consciously trying to seduce him, but the drug has released my inhibitions.

My body craves his touch. Craves satisfaction under his expert hands.

He straddles my waist. "What do you want me to do with you?"

The Gatekeeper

I moan, sounding wounded. "I want you to touch me."

He strokes a hand from my throat to my shoulder, then lower, to cradle my breast, which he squeezes roughly. "Like this?" He tugs the covers down to pinch my nipple into a tight bud. "How do you like to be touched, Kira?"

I shake my head. "Touch me...the way you want. The way you touched me last time. Before." I get confused about when our last time was.

He strokes his hand down my side and back up again. Lowers his head to suck my taut nipple. "You like it rough, Kira?"

"I didn't think so, but yes. I enjoyed it with you. I...I was afraid and liked it at the same time."

"Sometimes fear makes things more pleasurable," he observes between tongue flicks.

"That...doesn't make sense."

"No? You don't think fear could sharpen your senses? Make the pleasure more potent and the release more powerful?"

My hips buck as if he were already fucking me. I already require release.

He doesn't touch me roughly, despite my begging. Instead, he trails his fingertips lightly over my skin, making gooseflesh rise in his wake. He traces around my belly button, up between my breasts.

"Who makes you scream back home?" An air of danger shimmers around him, like he wants to kill every man I name.

When I moan, "No one," he relaxes.

"How do you think I should punish you for what you've done? For bugging the building? Giving our security information to the FBI?"

"Ohhh," I moan and arch, rocking my pelvis trying to find friction where I need it most.

"Hmm, *moya malen'kaya Valkiriya?*"

My legs swish under the covers like I'm swimming through an ocean of lust. I roll my head on the pillow. "I want you to punish me."

He chuckles. "Little warrior–it's a guarantee. I plan to punish you thoroughly. I just haven't decided how much will be pleasure and how much will be pain."

I work hard to focus on his face.

"Of course, there's always the possibility of withholding pleasure. Perhaps that would be the best angle with you. Hmm? Get you all riled up but never let you come? That seems a fitting punishment, doesn't it?"

"No-oo," I moan. I attempt to sit up. "I hate that. *Don't* do that."

He pushes me back down with a finger on my sternum. "You're in no position to negotiate."

"Maykl..."

He meets my gaze. I rub my lips together. "You can–you should...do whatever you want with me. I want you to do everything. Everything you want."

Oh God. Why can't I keep my mouth shut? I can't believe the shameful things pouring from my lips.

He lowers his head and flicks his tongue in my belly button, trailing it lower, pushing the covers down to reveal my bare legs. I part them wide for him, begging for it.

"You want my tongue here, little warrior?" He touches the tip of his tongue to the apex of my labia, wiggling it a little to delve inside. Just a hint of what it would feel like if he made himself at home there. If he sought out and licked and tortured the throbbing little nubbin that resides just below.

"Y-yes," I moan. "I want you to lick me there." I sound hoarse. I roll my head from side to side. "Oh God, why am I saying these things?"

"Because you owe me all your truths," Maykl says. "And I deserve them."

He's right. Or at least, in this moment, I feel that he's right. That I owe him a complete baring of my soul. There's no other way to win his pardon but to offer up everything I have to give: my body. My vulnerability.

I tricked him. Manipulated him. Betrayed his kindness.

Now I want him to take his due. Take from me everything he desires.

* * *

Maykl

Nikolai's advice to me changed everything.

Now, as I make Kira writhe beneath me, I know what's at stake. I know the bratva can't let her go. Not after her betrayal. So the only way to make this work is to make her want me.

Which means: *I might get to keep her.*

A chorus of bugles sound in my head at that thought.

The truth is that I haven't had that many women. The bratva cell in Moscow had prostitutes around. I gained quite a bit of experience with them in my teen years. They taught me how to pleasure a woman. Made sure I was well-versed in every variety of sexual positions, styles, and fantasies.

But I never had a woman who belonged to me. Of course, the bratva back in Russia forbade marriage or lasting relationships. No live-in girlfriends. Whores only is the rule.

It was the rule here with Ravil, too. At least until it wasn't. Until he knocked up a lawyer and then claimed her against her will.

Lucy loves him now, of course. And he's changed drastically now that baby Benjamin has come along. Most of the leadership in the Chicago bratva now have wives or girlfriends.

I want one, too.

I don't know what stopped me from going out and dating an American.

Perhaps the fact that it's too complicated to explain to an ordinary woman who I am and what I do. That the tattoos that mark my skin signify terrible sins.

That I'm wrapped up with an organization I can never leave.

The only way out is in a box, as they say.

It's hard to believe I could coax a woman to stick around.

Perhaps that's why the fantasy of keeping Kira trapped in my apartment forever is so enticing. A woman who can't walk out. Who won't leave me. Who has no choice but to stay with a man who has no soul.

I absolutely love hearing her spill her thoughts and feelings, with no ability to filter.

The temptation to use those pills on her again and again is already there. What man doesn't want to know everything the woman he wants is thinking? But, of course, it would be so wrong to use them to win her heart.

But is that what I actually want? To win this woman's heart? A woman I can't even trust?

But yes. Somewhere between the sex the first night and finding her digging through my drawers downstairs, I've become muddled. I've lost all touch with right and wrong.

Good and bad. Up from down. Perhaps I've been drugged too. Drugged by the scent of her skin, the touch of her silky moon-pale hair. The sound of her voice when she moans for more.

I want to give it all to her. I want to be her hero, her savior, and, yes, still her captor. Her jailor.

I want to be everything to her and have her be everything to me. I want to find her nephew and deliver him to her. Win her undying gratitude. At the same time, I want to force her to do all manner of depraved things. To be my slave. To service me. To receive my ministrations. To cry out my name every time she comes. This woman has bewitched me. This warrior has already cut out my heart. Now, all I have to do is make sure she doesn't leave with it. That shouldn't be too hard. I am the gatekeeper, after all. I am in charge of who enters and leaves this building.

And it's already been decided: Kira will never leave.

I reach up and pinch her nipple at the same moment I roll my tongue around her clit. She bucks, her hips lifting from the bed, her inner thighs shuddering, feet flailing.

I love her like this. Helpless. Needy. Greedy. I lift her knees up toward her shoulders to roll her up and open to me. Then I swirl my tongue around her anus.

She cries out. "Oh! *Gospodi!* That's so wrong! But it feels so good. What are you doing? Why are you doing that? Stop... I mean don't stop."

A better man would wait until the effects of the drug have left her system. But I am not a better man. I am her captor. And she is my prisoner. Besides, it is my job to make her fall in love. Which means I need to know everything she likes and doesn't like.

"You're going to take it back here today, little Valkyrie."

Her anus puckers and her hips jack up from the bed. "*Nyet*. No. Not...why?"

"It's your punishment."

"No, Maykl."

"You just told me you wanted me to do whatever I wanted to you. Didn't you?"

"Yes, but..."

"You're going to take me back here little warrior. You're going to take everything I've got to give you, and then you're going to beg me for more."

"Oh!" Her ice-blue eyes are wide, but the pupils are dilated, not contracted. And not from the drug. She's turned on.

I bring my mouth to her core, sucking on her nether lips and tracing my tongue inside them. Penetrating her with the tip. I flick it over her clit.

I stay at it until her moans have grown loud, and she's panting. Her thighs quiver and her knees press against my shoulders.

Then I release her and back off.

"No! Wait–" She reaches for me. "Where are you going?"

"I'm going to get a lubricant. You're going to lie there very quietly and wait for me. Understand?"

She nods her head rapidly.

"If you move from that bed, Kira, that tells me that you're not going to be a good prisoner for me. And if you're not going to be a good prisoner for me, I will have to turn you over to my bratva brothers. Do you want that?"

She shakes her head rapidly. "*Nyet*."

"Then don't move."

"I won't move," she promises.

I'm actually not certain how capable she is of moving. I

The Gatekeeper

know the drug relaxed her muscles. But she seemed to be regaining her strength.

It's a test. A risky one, probably. But I know if she comes out to fight me again, I can overpower her.

I'd love to build some trust between us. I don't want to keep her chained forever, as much as the thought turns me on. I want her to surrender.

I go to the kitchen. I don't have any conventional lubricant, but I know any food-grade vegetable oil will work. I find the small bottle of olive oil I keep in the cabinet and am satisfied when I return to find Kira has not moved an inch.

"Good girl," I purr as I crawl over her on the bed.

She eyes the olive oil bottle in my hand and searches my face.

I unscrew the lid and dribble a little bit on my fingers, then rub them over her slit. My fingers slide easily into her entrance, and she moans and rocks her pelvis to take me deeper. I stroke her inner walls, seeking her g-spot, and when I find the place where the tissue stiffens under my fingers, I pump against it.

When I rub my thumb over her clit at the same time, she comes, her inner walls spasming around my fingers, her cry filling the room.

"Good girl. That's how you take it," I encourage.

I slide my fingers out and roll her to her belly. She lets me move her, which is the biggest turn-on of all.

That my warrior has gone docile. She's given herself to me.

I grab a pillow and scoop an arm under her waist to lift her hips and stuff it beneath them. "Spread your legs, *Valkiriya*."

She obeys.

I drizzle a thin line of olive oil along the crack of her ass then start massaging. I take my time, stroking between her cheeks, sliding down to rub her clit then around her anus.

I add more oil and give her a butt massage, then spank her pert ass, alternating right and left without holding back.

She gasps and cries out but holds still for it, parting her legs even wider, like it turns her on.

"Do you like that, *Valkiriya*?" I ask, remembering that she can't lie.

"I...yes." She rubs her face against the pillow she hugged when I rolled her over. "Or...*like* it isn't the right word. I don't like it, but it gets me hot. I want more."

I fucking love the honesty from her. I don't know how long it will last, but I want to wring every last truth from her beautiful lips.

I deliver another dozen slaps then rub and massage her ass some more.

"I like punishing you," I admit, giving her a dose of my own honesty. "I like the little cries and gasps you give me. I like taking it just past the line of too much." She tips her ass back at me, and I drag my thumb along her crack until it comes to press against her anus.

"How do you know?"

"Years of practice. But at a much more unpleasant kind of torture."

I breach her back hole with my thumb and massage the oil inside and around the tight ring of muscles.

She whimpers and mewls. With my thumb still inside her ass, I slap her ass a few times. Then I remove my thumb and unbutton my jeans.

Kira looks over her shoulder at me, beautiful and bold. She watches as I pull off my shirt. She still embodies the warrior energy, even naked, beneath me, in this ignominious position.

"You will take me," I tell her firmly, and she doesn't protest. She just turns her face back to the pillow, resting on her forearms, the cords along her back tightening in anticipation.

I stroke my cock with the oil, making sure there is plenty of lubrication before I press the head against her back entrance.

"Push, Kira. Push to open to me."

She makes an adorable little sound as she obeys, and I'm in. I go slowly until the head makes it through, then press in deep. Her shoulders hunch and she goes completely still.

I fist her silky blonde hair and tug her head gently back. "Relax, *Valkiriya*. Open to me. Breathe."

Her back softens.

I work slowly in and out of her, giving her time to stretch and grow accustomed to my size.

She moans and mewls every time I move, whimpering.

"That's it." The pleasure starts to overtake me. I forget about being gentle as my own need grows.

I pump into her, bracing my weight on one hand, still fisting her hair in the other.

"This is where you take it when you've been a bad girl."

"Yes, okay." She gasps her agreement.

Flames of heat lick through me. My breath rasps in and out like I've run up every flight of stairs in the Kremlin.

"Maykl? Oh...it's...I need..."

"What do you need, *moya malen'kaya Valkiriya*?"

She reaches her hand beneath her to touch between her legs.

Knowing she's turned on, that she's seeking her own release clitorally, drives me wild. I have to remember not to be too rough as I thrust in and out, pounding down the home stretch.

"Maykl....Maykl."

Blyad'. I absolutely love hearing her choke out my name in that hoarse, desperate voice.

My balls draw up tight, and then it's right on top of me. Like a tidal wave is pushing me forward, I'm launched into climax. I come inside her, pressing deep and delivering a series of short thrusts until I'm finished.

Only then do I remember to help my Valkyrie. I slip my hand under her hips and tangle my fingers over hers, rubbing her clit. She directs them down, pressing them inside her to feel her orgasm, the muscles squeezing and releasing.

"Yes."

She said it, but I could say the same.

Best orgasm of my life.

I nuzzle against her, kissing the back of her neck, and nibbling her ear.

Her slender back still heaves with her slowing pants. A layer of sweat slicks the surface between us.

I ease out. "Come." I scoop her into my arms. "Let's get you cleaned up."

She loops her arms around my neck. "I can't move," she complains.

"I'll hold you up."

In the bathroom, I set her on her feet while I turn on the water, then hold her trembling hand as she steps in, and I step in after her.

To my surprise and pleasure, she turns to face me, letting me gather her up in my arms and hold her close under the spray of water.

We stay like that for a long time. Until her heartbeat has slowed, and she draws a deep breath and sighs.

I pick up a bar of soap and take my time, sudsing her

The Gatekeeper

with long, slow strokes, turning washing into a sensuous exploration of her every curve. Every cranny.

Her hands coast over my body, too. She traces my tattoos. Brushes her lips over my hairy chest. Uses her teeth on my pectoral muscle. "I've never been with a man like you," she says.

I don't know whether it's still the drug making her talk or if this truth has been won honestly from her.

I don't care.

"What kind of man?" I use the shampoo to suds her hair.

"I don't know. You are just...different. Everything I thought I'd hate but found out I love."

I know she's not saying she loves me. That would be absurd to believe I've already won her heart.

But the beginnings of the feeling must be there, or she wouldn't have said it. She's capable of loving me, perhaps. The ingredients for love are present.

Or maybe she's just talking about sex.

Which, for now, is enough.

And that's when I finally remember there's one thing that could doom this whole thing. Bring everything crashing down around my ears.

Kira doesn't know what I've done.

She doesn't know that I'm the man who killed her father.

And when she finds that out, no amount of sex will save me.

Or her.

Chapter Eleven

Kira

I don't know what's wrong with me. It must still be the effects of the drug in my system. I should be engaged in hand-to-hand combat with Maykl right now. Fighting for my life. Trying to escape this prison.

Instead, I'm sitting across from Maykl at the tiny two-person kitchen table that sits in front of the picture window. My muscles are still loose. My body sated.

Soon, my stomach will be, as well. "Roasted salmon with caramelized cauliflower and broccolini or braised short ribs with wilted arugula?" Maykl pauses in dishing the gourmet dinner from the to-go containers they came in onto plates to look at me. "Or a little of both?"

"Salmon, please," I say.

This feels more like a date than captivity, despite the fact that I'm sitting here naked with handcuffs on my wrists.

And I suppose that's the main reason I'm not fighting.

Some part of me doesn't want to run away. No matter how hard my brain keeps trying to convince me that I'm a dead woman, that I may never see beyond the confines of this apartment again.

I want to be with Maykl. To explore this dangerous, unconventional relationship we have.

He doesn't seem like a psychopath or a killer, though the tattoos prove otherwise. Bottom line? He sees me for who I am.

I know that for certain because I told him everything when I took the drug he gave me. He absorbed it all and still gave me two orgasms. Still brought me into the shower and washed me with so much care it made me want to weep.

Embarrassingly, I did weep. And then I told him why I wept. I confessed that no one had ever taken such care of me. That after my dad was murdered, my mom became severely depressed, and Anya was the only person who looked out for me.

He said very little, but he didn't stop. He washed my hair and rinsed me. Toweled me dry. Then he wrapped me in a blanket, handcuffed me to the bed, and handed me the remote to the television.

What did I tell him? I remember the words pouring out of me without any filter. I told him about the FBI. The bugs. The security code. I'd confessed...

Oh boy.

Did I actually say I wanted him to punish me?

Thinking of it makes my core heat. I must be crazy. I cannot be enjoying this scenario. What total insanity.

What had he said?

I plan to punish you thoroughly. I just haven't decided how much will be pleasure and how much will be pain.

It must have been the drug that made those words heat my body to the temperature of molten lava. It certainly can't be that I crave that sort of treatment at his hands. That I desire that rough but attentive way he has with me.

Things could be far worse. I've been captured by a dangerous but attractive man who is more interested in sexual torture than anything bloody or painful.

Now, after leaving me alone for a couple of hours, he's had dinner delivered and is acting like a perfect gentleman–other than the handcuffs and his refusal to allow me to wear clothes.

The smell of the food makes my stomach rumble. I didn't realize how hungry I am. Maykl slides the plate in front of me. Despite being transported, the food retained visual appeal, with a slice of lemon and sprig of rosemary atop the salmon.

Maykl stands over me, hesitating. "Can I trust you with a fork, little warrior? Probably not."

"I'm too hungry to fight," I tell him, unable to take my eyes off the food. My mouth waters for it.

He tsks. "If only I could believe you. But I think the truth serum is out of your bloodstream now. I can't trust anything that comes from those pretty lips."

He retrieves the other plate of food and one fork and sits down beside me. "I don't mind feeding you, though. In fact, I rather enjoy it." He forks a piece of salmon and holds it out to me.

I take the morsel into my mouth and moan softly at its perfection. Lightly salted and herbed, crispy on the outside, tender on the inside, it's delicious.

I watch as he takes a bite of his own food. He doesn't make me wait long for my next bite.

I should hate him for reducing me to eating from his hand. Or better yet–I should feel nothing. Should be able to keep emotions out of this scenario so my mind can work out how to escape, but I'm still in some kind of surrendered state to him.

He finds feeding me pleasurable. I find eating from his hand equally satisfying. Like I'm proving the bond we forged. The one he doesn't trust yet. I tell myself it's a manipulation, but that's a lie.

I'm doing it for him.

For me.

For us.

I do feel bonded to this man. I trust him with my body. Trust him to pleasure me. Now, to feed me and care for me.

I've had to rely on myself and myself alone for most of my life. Now I have no choice but to rely on Maykl for even my most basic needs. I both hate and love the way it feels. Terrifying. Like I'm falling from a precipice, and I'm hurtling through the air. The rush of the wind and the sense of soaring are exhilarating, but I don't know whether I'll reach the cushion of water or the destruction of rock when I touch down.

He continues to feed me, eating his own dinner between bites until we both are finished. Then he picks up the plates and fork, washes them, and returns with a bottle of water, which he uncaps and hands to me.

I wash the dinner down and use a napkin to wipe my lips.

"What's happening, Maykl? What are you doing with me?"

Maykl towers over me. "I'm keeping you, Kira. And if you prove you can't be kept... well, then..." He shrugs and leaves a space for me to fill in the blank.

"Well, then, what?"

He sinks into the chair beside me. "You won't walk free. Not as an enemy of this cell."

My heart pounds in my chest. I knew this had to be the case, yet hearing him say it makes it solid and real.

A sheen of tears coats my eyes, but I blink them back. "So I must prove...what? That I'll be your pet?"

He holds my gaze. Neither of us moves. I can't breathe.

When he shakes his head, there's regret there. "I don't want you to get hurt, Kira."

My lips tremble. I don't think it's from fear. It's more like my feelings are hurt although that's absurd. But it's true. It hurts to have Maykl threaten me, unembellished though the threat may be.

I nod, bitterness twisting my lips. "So, you keep me until you have no further use for me, and then I'm dead?"

He winces. "*Nyet*. No. Not like that. I've been charged with your keeping. If you escape, I'm dead. We both are. We're saddled with each other now. We might as well make the best of it, no?"

"Where's my phone? I will need to check in with my boss, or he will know something's wrong."

"We have it."

Something in the way he says it gives me the feeling they will be using it to set a trap for the FBI.

"I will need to check in with my boss or else he will think something's amiss."

"We're handling it."

Yep. I was right. This is bad. If they fight the FBI, good people could get hurt. Plus, the FBI will think I'm a double agent, and I'll never get the information I need on Mika. I need to try to stop this.

I blink at him. "How can you live this way? You are in constant fear for your life. What's the reward? This nice apartment? Enough money to buy a fancy meal?"

"No. Brotherhood is the reward. Protection and power.

Family. Belonging. But you already know–once you're in, you're in for life."

"We could escape. Together." It's probably too soon to suggest it, but I have to try.

He doesn't even consider it, though. He shakes his head. "I would never betray my brothers. Nor will I allow you to harm my family."

"Your loyalty is misplaced. These people aren't your family. If you're afraid for your life–"

"We live by a code. The code is honored, or there are consequences. I don't live in fear. I'm proud of what I've become."

Something about that statement, and the clear, confident way he holds my gaze shakes me to my core. Maykl is a criminal. His crimes are marked all over his skin. Yet he conducts himself with honor, holds himself with pride. And I don't think it's from a warped sense of self. I do think he's an honorable man, in his own way.

He's protected me, even as his prisoner.

And that dislodges something at the very bottom of the foundation of my case against the bratva. A pebble that stopped up the drain rolls aside, and the basin of hate begins to leak its contents. To slip away. Because how can I reconcile my belief that the bratva is all bad when this man before me is fundamentally...good?

It makes me want to be more like him. He has clearly suffered traumas, same as I have. Yet he's come out of them with a strength and resiliency. I guess I have, too, but there's an underlying bitterness, anger, and hate behind my strength. Maykl is rooted in generosity and brotherhood. Unlike me, who resisted and refused all human bonds after my painful past, Maykl seems to have forged strong ones, and they clearly have made him what he is.

The Gatekeeper

I think again about how he stood in the doorway of that pottery studio marveling over the art involved in creating a pot. It's such a small thing, and yet it shows a depth. He's capable of contemplation. Of appreciation.

"I want to learn to throw pots," I blurt.

Maykl's eyebrows raise in surprise. "That can be arranged," he says slowly. "You will have to earn it as a privilege, though."

That's when the anxiety simmering inside me goes quiet. As if the simple privilege of being allowed to learn to shape clay changes everything.

But it says so much. It says I have a future of some kind. There's something beyond these four walls and Maykl's bed. And…I'm eager to explore it.

* * *

Maykl

Ravil texts me during dinner to say that Kira's nephew is with Vlad. The bratva boss is protective of his adopted son. He wished to speak with Mika to see if he wanted any contact with her.

I hold this information back for the time being.

Kira remained surprisingly docile through dinner, even after I informed her she can't leave. I can't decide if she's trying to play me again. But no, she never fooled me before. Right from the beginning, I knew there was something off about her helpless female act followed by the blatant seduction.

Now, something about her seems more real. The truth serum made her drop her walls with me. Or else it's still in her system, but I'd prefer to think that isn't what wrought the change.

I lead her to the couch, and we sit down together. I wrap a blanket around her and arrange her next to me, pulling her close to my side with her legs over my lap.

"Is cuddling required?" There's a light softness to her teasing I haven't heard before.

"Yes," I say gruffly.

She leans into me and rests her head on my shoulder. "I don't mind."

I kiss her hair.

I give her the remote, and she scrolls through the options for a long time, as if nothing will satisfy her. Or perhaps she's just not used to the choices on American television.

Eventually, she stops on *Bridgerton*, a historical soap opera of some kind, which seems an odd choice. I would expect my little warrior to pick something suspenseful. Or even a horror film. I don't protest. Maybe she's trying to annoy me with something she thinks I'll hate.

But no, she seems completely absorbed.

Which makes me absorb it, as well.

We watch the first episode through to the end, both of us sitting in silence, seemingly riveted to the story. As if it might tell us something about our current situation. About each other or our relationship.

It rolls into a second episode, then a third.

When Kira yawns, I take the remote and turn off the television. "Let's go to bed, *moya Valkiriya*."

We stand together in the bathroom, brushing our teeth, like the most ordinary of couples. Well, except for the handcuffs. Maybe some ordinary couples use those, too. Probably not for brushing teeth, though.

In bed, I unlock the cuffs and attach one to my wrist for the night. After I turn off the light, I tell her the news.

"My *pakhan* knows where your nephew is."

She goes still, waiting for more.

"What will you do for the information?"

"A-anything."

That was what I suspected. "You chose the wrong side."

She remains silent.

I guess I want her to say it. To be sorry she worked against us, but of course, that's foolish. Just because we can locate her nephew doesn't erase the wrongs that were done to her by the bratva.

And no gift I give her could cancel out what I took from her on my initiation night into the bratva.

I reach for her in the darkness. Find the curve of her cheek with my hand and caress it. "Be good, little warrior, and I'll give you what you want."

It's cruel of me to try to win her allegiance this way, but I already know it can be bought. It was with this promise that her supervisor convinced her to help the Moscow bratva get past our defenses. Of course, she believed she was helping the FBI.

"What do you need me to do?" she whispers in the dark. She thinks I will ask for some deed. A double-cross of the "FBI" perhaps.

Of course, we already have that planned without her help.

But it's good to know I have enough leverage if we do need her.

"Just be good," I murmur, stroking her cheek with my thumb.

"Mmm." She makes a little sound of consideration like she's trying to figure out what that means.

How could she know that I'm trying to negotiate for her love? To win her permanent allegiance? But perhaps giving her Mika will do that. When she learns he has been well cared for, as a real, adopted son, not as a young bratva brigadier, maybe she'll think differently of us.

"He is safe and happy. His adopted father will ask him if he wants to see you."

She sucks in a shocked breath. "Where is he? Who adopted him?"

"No. You haven't earned your answers yet. I don't owe you this."

She lets out a little sob of breath. "I don't know if I can even believe you."

"You will have to decide, won't you? Who you can trust, and who is feeding you lies."

She falls quiet. Her fingertips find my chest, and she traces the contours in the darkness. "It feels wrong to trust you." Her words hit me like a blow until she adds, "But I think I do."

Guilt mingles with satisfaction. What will happen to this trust when she finds out I'm the man who pulled the trigger on her dad?

I want to tell her. No, I don't want to tell her, but I know I should. Just get it out right now to see if there's any possibility of moving past it.

But I'm savoring this moment too much. I can't bring myself to snap this tenuous gossamer thread that's reaching between our hearts and connecting them right now.

Chapter Twelve

Kira

I sleep heavily. When I wake, I'm bound to Maykl's bed. The covers have been tucked around my naked body, so I'm not cold. I appear to be alone.

I listen for a moment but hear nothing. A laptop is open on the dresser with a tiny green light shining at the top.

A camera.

He's monitoring me, possibly from his desk downstairs.

Gospodi, how long have I been asleep? I try to swallow, but my mouth is dry.

I lift my head and try to appear pathetic as I focus on the tiny dot on the laptop screen. "Maykl? I'm thirsty." I don't exaggerate my desperation. I actually trust that he will come. "I need water."

Just a few minutes later, I hear him enter the apartment. I hear the clink of a glass, then a faucet runs. When he comes in, he stands over me with a glass of water in his hand.

He wears a wicked smirk, and instead of bringing the water glass to my lips, he twitches the blanket down to reveal my naked form. "*Valkiriya.* I like having you chained to my bed." He cups the back of my head to help lift it as he brings the glass to my lips.

Water dribbles out both sides of my mouth when he spills it too quickly. He dries it with his thumb. "Do you need to use the bathroom?"

I nod, and he pulls out the key to the handcuffs and fits it in the lock.

I consider fighting. I could take him by surprise the moment he unlocks my wrists. I have my strength back completely. I'm no longer softened by the drug and the sex and the vulnerability he wrenched from me yesterday.

Our gazes lock, and I know he knows exactly what I'm thinking. His movements still. He's ready for any attack. I probably wouldn't win against him although he's reluctant to hurt me, which I could use to my advantage.

But then, I might be reluctant to hurt him, too, now.

"I'll be good," I murmur, realizing that it's true.

For the moment, anyway.

He says he knows where Mika is. I think I believe him. And, also, I'm...not hating my captivity. If I bide my time, there may be an easier way to get free.

That's what I tell myself. It's not that I want to remain Maykl's prisoner indefinitely. Not at all.

He releases the cuffs from the bed and tips his head toward the bathroom. I use the toilet and wash my face. When I emerge, he's not in the bedroom.

I do a quick sweep of the room, looking for a weapon. There aren't many. The bedside lamp, perhaps. But once more, I choose against fighting. Just note it for use in the future, if necessary.

And for some reason, I'm feeling more and more that it won't be necessary.

The Gatekeeper

I find Maykl in the kitchen. He's poured Life cereal into a bowl for me. He adds milk and offers a spoon. I sit in the same place as yesterday and eat with my manacled hands. It's not easy, but not impossible, either.

I decide not to complain. I'm being good for him. Seeing where that gets me.

Every moment that goes by, I sense the impending sense of disaster. Soon, the FBI and Stepanov will arrive, and the bratva will be waiting for them. Considering the FBI will think I'm a double agent, I can't count on either side protecting me when it goes down, and that's a problem. Even more of a problem? I'm starting to align myself with the bad guys. I'm becoming that double agent.

When I finish eating, Maykl takes me back to the bedroom, where he chains me, spread eagle in the center of his bed. A feverish heat blooms, just at the position.

Knowing he put me in this position for his pleasure.

He traces the curves of my body with a heavy-lidded gaze. "Did you like telling me all your deepest fantasies yesterday, Kira?"

"I didn't tell all of them." I say it like a dare. Like I want him to find out the rest of them.

He takes my bait. "Then I will have to pry the rest of them from you."

My pulse skitters. Belly flip-flops with excitement. "How?"

"I'm going to make you beg and plead and scream, little warrior." He tweaks one nipple between the knuckles of two fingers. "But I think that's what you want, isn't it?"

"*Nyet*," I lie.

"We'll see." He's smug. Very sure of himself. The secrets he stole from me gave him confidence.

A sliver of warning rings through me. I believe this man

is sane. Not sociopathic. But I may have given him more credit than he deserves. After all, he is a killer, and he works for the bratva. He may have a very skewed sense of right and wrong.

Also, just because he doesn't want to hurt me doesn't mean he'll ever let me go.

He pulls the covers completely off me and crawls between my legs. His breath feathers hot across my lady bits.

He presses a chaste kiss to the apex of my nether lips, and a shudder of desire rolls through me.

I'm already close to begging, and he hasn't even begun. The tip of his tongue parts me, and he rolls it over my clit.

"Does it bother you, Kira?"

My inner thighs tremble, straining against the zip ties. "Wh-what?" I warble as he sucks one of my labia into his mouth then releases it with a pop.

"To receive pleasure from someone you hate. A bratva brother?"

For some reason, that statement brings a sharp stab of pain to my chest. A protest to my lips. Because my hatred has already mingled with attraction. With desire. My need to best the bratva is caught up on the hooks of attraction. Of interest in this big, burly man who seems so very interested in me.

Not just in the information I gave him. But in me.

"My hate..." I can't go on because I feel it jamming up under my ribs, pressing against my lungs to constrict my breath. It's old. Finely honed. Born of the fear and helplessness of my youth. Of a desire to overcome that feeling once and for all.

It doesn't help that Maykl has begun to lave me with his

tongue, to penetrate me with the tip of it, to screw one finger inside of me.

"You see?" He lifts his head and smirks, his lips glossy with my juices. "You can't even answer me."

"You are part of something I hate," I manage to say. It's the most I can offer. I can't say I *don't* hate him because he's in it, he represents it. But no part of me feels hate directly toward him.

He's too...

"*Ugn.*" I throw my head back with the shock of pleasure he delivers when he finds my G-spot.

Too...

Another whine leaves my lips. "*Pozhaluysta.*" I'm begging, just as he predicted.

"Tell me what you need, *Valkiriya.*"

I tug at my bonds, lust, and helplessness making me aggressive. Angry. "I need you to set me free."

He shakes his head. "Not going to happen." He slaps between my legs, delivering several light spanks that make me yank even harder to be free.

Then, to my horror, he backs away, off the bed. "I'll let you simmer a while. I have to get back to my station."

"Wait!" I cry in alarm. "I'm hungry! Thirsty! I have to go to the bathroom!"

None of those things are true. I just don't want to be left alone. Not when I'm hot and needy and have no means of finishing myself off.

He seems to know it's a bluff because he just offers a shrug. "You'll have to think very hard about how to please me next time."

"Wait...what?"

He walks out the door, and I stare in fury, mouth open, frustration slamming through me.

Evil man. Wicked, horrible, marvelous demon of a man.

I suck in a shaky breath and let it out with a moan. Maybe I do hate him after all.

If he keeps this up, I will definitely learn to thoroughly despise him.

* * *

Maykl

The trouble with torturing Kira is that I'm torturing myself at the same time. I leave the guards in front of my door to watch the apartment and go back to my station with the biggest set of blue balls in history.

I left Gleb in charge of the front door. "You back already? Go," he waves me off. "I'm here. You go do whatever it is that has you occupied today. I have nothing else to do."

I hesitate. Leaving Kira alone was part of my plan although it's true that I didn't want to leave her for long. But the funeral home left a message on my phone saying her sister's ashes were ready to be picked up, so I could run that errand.

"Thank you." I speak English because that's Ravil's rule for us. If he didn't make it, none of us would perfect our English since we all live here together.

I text Ravil to make sure he won't nail me to a wall over leaving the building, and he calls me.

"Kira's phone has proved useful," he tells me.

"It has? Good."

"Stepanov set a meet time for her. We will be there to take them down."

I note that Ravil doesn't tell me when and where. Like

he doesn't trust me not to betray them. Like I might choose Kira over my brothers.

Would I?

Love can make men do strange things. I've watched the behavior of my brothers change radically when they chose a woman.

"How is it going with her?"

I think of my beautiful Valkyrie bound to my bed, and my cock thickens. "I'm making progress."

"Maxim advised you to win her heart."

"Yes."

"Can you?"

I swallow. Can I? The possibility is there. But there's the issue of her father's death. That may be an insurmountable issue.

"I want to," I answer. The only answer I can give.

"Good. Then get the ashes. Take care of your female. We'll handle the security of the building until things are resolved."

"Understood. Thank you, *Pakhan*."

With his blessing, I pick up the ashes and then stop for soup and sandwiches from the deli on the corner. I buy lunch for Gleb while I'm there, dropping it at the desk for him when I walk by.

He lifts his chin in a gruff version of thanks.

I take the stairs up and enter the apartment.

I set the lunch down in the kitchen then head into the bedroom. The moment I see Kira, I forget all about eating. About breathing. About doing anything but devouring her.

Her cheeks are flushed. Nipples puckered. The flesh between her legs lifts and flutters in anticipation of being touched. She looks magnificent.

I lean against the dresser to take in the sight. To keep

myself from going straight to her and ravishing her in every way possible. Because this is supposed to be punishment.

I'm making her wait for it.

I watch her closely. If I saw any fear in her, I'd probably go some other way. But all I see is irritation and desire.

She wants this. She probably hates that she wants it, but that doesn't change the way she writhes on the bed, panting. The way she pleads with her eyes.

I saunter over and climb on the bed. "Shall we try again?" I slide my hands under her ass and squeeze it as I lick into her once more. She's even juicier than she was when I left, as if her desire has only grown each minute I was gone.

I pause when she doesn't answer, and she quickly barks out a "*Da.*"

I reward her with several firm strokes of my tongue, ending with a slow roll around her clit.

She rocks her hips up to my mouth. "Is this your fantasy, Maykl?" she pants.

"Yes."

"Have you done it before?"

Is she jealous? "What? Captured FBI informants and punished them with my tongue? No."

She shimmies her hips from side to side. "Have you done this with other women?"

She *is* jealous. Smugness zips through me.

I lift my head and grin. "No. You're the first woman to inspire this precise treatment. Does that please you, Kira?"

I'm sure that it does because her cheeks turn pink as our gazes tangle.

"I'm tempted to torture you this way all day long," I say.

"Don't leave me again!" she cries out in alarm, and I chuckle.

The Gatekeeper

"No? I crawl over her, unbuttoning my pants. "What do you need, little warrior? You want more than my tongue between your legs?"

"Y-yes please," she warbles. She's adorable when she's coming undone like this.

I grab a condom from my nightstand and shuck my clothes before rolling it on.

I consider her. "Do I leave you in this position?" I muse aloud.

But I already know. As pretty as she looks splayed out that way, I want those legs wrapped around me when I sink deep inside her. I want her to be able to respond to me.

I unlock both her ankles and one of her wrists, then I climb over her and pause, looking down. I suppose I'm waiting for consent, even though she just begged me for it. But I want to feel wanted.

"I want on top," she whispers.

I smile. How like her. My little warrior, demanding what she wants.

I release her wrist from where it's chained to the bed and attach the other cuff to my wrist. Then I roll to my back, my hands at her waist to help her climb on.

Her eyes roll back in her head as she climbs on. Her internal muscles give me a squeeze, making me shudder with pleasure.

I watch as she takes what she needs from me, starting slow, her body moving in beautiful, graceful undulations. Soon her hips begin to snap as she tries to take me deeper. She picks up her pace, loses her breath. She braces both her hands on my shoulders, and I use my free hand to urge her hips forward.

She starts chanting. Babbling. Things like "now" and "yes" and "please". She cries out my name twice. Each time sends a surge of lust through me. On the third time, I can't take it anymore. I flip her onto her back and pound to our glorious finish. We both come at the same time–her muscles milking my dick for every last drop.

I shudder and shake and groan with the release.

And when stillness descends, I lower my lips to her neck and kiss there. "Thank you," I murmur.

She lets out a small cry, like my thanks wounded her. When I lift my head, there are tears in her eyes. She blinks them rapidly away, turning her face to the side.

I catch her jaw and turn it back. "What is it?"

"I don't know," she says, and I believe her. "It was just... intense. But good, Maykl. So good." After a moment's hesitation, she says, "Thank you." Almost like it costs her to offer the thanks.

Like she's admitting something to herself when she gives it.

I claim a soft kiss from her lips. The kind without tongue that moves across the surface and squeezes at the end.

She lets out another tiny, pained cry.

My tenderness wounds her again.

I intend to keep wounding her this way. Showing her kindness. Offering my presence. Maybe eventually, she'll learn to take it without it hurting.

Chapter Thirteen

K*ira*

After we shower, Maykl lets me put on some clothes. He has me uncuffed but keeps me within grabbing distance.

"I picked up your sister's ashes," he tells me.

The sensation of a swallowed stone in my stomach that I always have when I think of Anya returns. "Oh." I can't think of anything to say. "Where are they?"

He points to the cardboard cylinder on his desk.

I walk over and open the lid then quickly replace it. I'm not squeamish, but something about knowing what's inside creeps me out.

"Do you...want to keep them? Or scatter them as a farewell?"

I look out Maykl's giant windows toward the lake.

"Maybe...scatter them. Out there. Leave her to Chicago."

He nods. "I'll arrange it." He pulls out his phone to text something.

I can't help it. I throw myself at him, wrapping my arms around his sturdy trunk and squeezing hard.

It's hard to fathom why he's being so kind. What he could possibly hope to gain by carrying me through this.

He kisses the top of my head. A message comes through on his phone, which he checks and then pockets. "Get your boots and coat. We're going now."

"To the lake?" I blink in surprise.

"Yes."

"I can go out? I mean, we're going out to the lake?" I'm having a hard time assimilating this fact. That I could go from prisoner to pampered in just the blink of an eye.

"Even in war, there's time given to bury the dead."

"Are we at war?" I ask. Because I no longer want to be.

I want to find some way out of this situation that leaves us both on the same side. But is that even possible?

He tilts his head. "We are until we aren't anymore. Go and put on your boots."

I mull over his words as I pull on my boots and coat. When I return, he hands me the ashes then shows me the screen of his phone.

I gasp. *Mika.*

All grown up. I don't know how I even recognize him, except the family resemblance is there. He looks like my sister.

"In case you need an incentive not to give me trouble." I think I catch a tinge of regret in Maykl's face as he makes the threat.

My eyes water and I press my lips together and nod. "He's safe?"

"He's fine. I'm not threatening his safety. I'm telling you to be good, so you can see him."

I bob my head, still overcome with emotion. The relief

that he's actually been found–that he's still alive and Maykl knows where–makes me want to drop to my knees and praise a god I don't even believe in.

Maykl sees my emotion and loops an arm around me to lead me to the door. Outside stand two battle-faced bratva soldiers. I absorb that information. I've had additional guards at the door this whole time.

For some reason, it doesn't daunt me. I don't feel as concerned about making an escape.

We are until we aren't anymore.

There's a riddle in there. Something to work out. Some clue about what he's planning for me.

"Follow us," Maykl commands, and the guards tag along into the elevator. Someone else sits behind Maykl's desk. An older man but clearly still bratva based on the tattoos that extend beyond his sleeves and across the backs of his hands.

Maykl keeps his arm around me. I'm sure it's to keep me close, to make sure I don't run, but it also feels protective. Comforting, even.

He leads me out to the sidewalk toward the lake. As we pass by the window of the building, I hear a knock and Kat gives me a friendly wave from her studio.

I smile back because it's impossible not to return the friendliness.

It's cold out, and I tighten the jacket around me as we walk into the wind. Maykl leads me to the end of a dock. I stand and stare out at the water for a long time. It's a dark blue. The sky is grey to match the occasion.

Maykl doesn't hurry me. Or lead. He just stands beside me, his hulk and strength giving me a pillar to lean into.

I take a deep breath. "Okay, let's do this." I open the lid

of the ashes container and unceremoniously dump the whole thing. No scattering. Just a straight pour.

"May the earth be soft for her." Maykl speaks the traditional Russian saying.

"Except she's in water," I say. I start to laugh. It's a hysterical kind of laugh. The sort that could just as easily turn to tears. In fact, some tears do stream down my cheeks as I knock into Maykl's solid form, rocking on my feet with hysteria.

He wraps me into his arms and sways with me gently as I laugh until I sob.

When the outburst finally dies, I pull away and wipe my tears. "I'm okay," I say, even though he said nothing.

Behind him, the soldiers stand stoic and watchful.

I turn back to the water, to the swirls of ashes stretching away into the giant body of water. "Bye Anya." I swallow. "I'm sorry I didn't do more to help you. I'm sorry you were a shitty mom. I'm sorry you're dead. I'm sorry...I'm sorry it wasn't me."

Maykl visibly flinches. "What does that mean?" he demands.

I don't look at him. I keep my gaze on the trail of ashes growing longer as it stretches further and further away. "I mean when the bratva came. I could've taken her place. I wouldn't have let it break me the way it broke her."

Maykl's brows draw together. "You...you feel guilty they chose her?"

I nod.

He moves closer, standing right beside me, my shoulder against his arm as we look out together.

"We all wish there were things we could change about our past. Things we've done. Things done to us. Unforgivable things. But that guilt serves no one."

"I can't just put it away. If I did, I'd stop caring. And I feel like I barely care for anyone or anything anymore." Tears clog my voice.

"I..." Maykl seems to be struggling. "There's something I've done, Kira. After I killed my father. I don't regret that crime. He would have killed me if I didn't defend myself. But I didn't understand how it worked. The *pakhan* made me believe the brotherhood would take me in." Maykl waits so long to speak that I know he must be wrestling with his memories.

"But they require initiation. A price to pay to become one of them." He shifts away from me, like he doesn't want to contaminate me with his crimes. "I didn't know what a cost that initiation would have on my soul."

I finally turn. He's pulled me completely out of my own turmoil. The need to comfort him rises–a surprising but sweet sensation.

"What was it?" I ask softly.

He faces me and works to swallow. His eyes are haunted. "An execution. A man who owed them money and tried to pay with counterfeit currency. I was–" he draws a breath. "Thirteen years old. They put a gun in my hand and pointed me at him. I had to prove myself. If I didn't...I'd be on my own."

I reach over and pick up his hand on the rail of the dock. "Not your only killing, though, right?" I trace the X's on his knuckles.

He shakes his head. "No, but...the one that ruined me."

I feel the heaviness and constriction of his statement like a cloud of darkness in my lungs. "You're not ruined."

Somehow, I'm sure. Absolutely positive.

But he shakes his head. "You don't know." He looks so pained. I squeeze his fingers. "You don't know who it was."

I suck in a sharp breath suddenly picturing the worst. A child or old lady. Someone completely defenseless. "Were they innocent?"

"No. He was mixed up with bratva business. He tried to cheat his way out of his debts, I was told. And it wasn't the first time." Maykl searches my face. What he seeks, I don't know. I feel the magnitude of it, though.

He's not doing a great job of cheering me up, if that was his intent.

I blink back tears. For him. For me. For Anya and Mika. "Why are you telling me this?"

He drops his head and shakes it. "I lost the point. I meant to tell you that guilt serves no one. My guilt can't change what I did. Questioning that choice won't change it. Nor will stopping myself from experiencing the rest of this life. The guilt serves no one. It doesn't bring back the dead. It doesn't heal any wounds–it only makes them fester.

"So you were thirteen when you joined the bratva?" I ask.

"Yes."

Thirteen. The same age I was when Anya was taken by the bratva to pay my father's debt.

"You were just a kid. You didn't know any other way out of your situation." I nod. "You did what you had to do to survive."

Maybe I was wrong. Maybe I would've died inside if the bratva had taken me instead. Sought out drugs to numb the pain, the way Anya did. To believe I would've done better is naive at best, arrogant at worst.

Besides, Maykl's right. The guilt doesn't bring back the dead.

I can only move forward. Live in the present.

I tug his hand. My fingers are chapped and numb in the

cold. I have gloves in my pockets but didn't bother putting them on. "Let's go back. It's done."

Maykl clasps my hand in his, and then slides it into the pocket of his leather bomber jacket.

We walk back to the building in silence. Together. Apart. Somehow entwined in a way I don't understand.

In this moment, I don't need to understand it. I'm content to just walk by this man's side. Receive his warmth and strength. The vulnerability he just offered me to match my own.

For the moment, I'm going to surrender. He knows where Mika is. He showed me a picture.

Maybe everything led me to this moment. To exactly where I'm supposed to be. In some cosmic arrangement of our fates, I was taken prisoner by the one person who could help me.

And then I feel Anya. Not the pitiful woman who overdosed, but young Anya. The one who tried to protect us both with a butcher knife.

She had warrior energy then. Same as mine.

And it feels like she's here with me now. Right by my side.

It feels like a promise that everything is going to be okay.

* * *

Maykl

I'm reluctant to put Kira back in the handcuffs when we return to my apartment. She stands at the window for a while, looking out at the lake, and then she walks into my kitchen and starts opening cupboards.

"What are you looking for?"

"I want to bake," she declares. "Anya is the one who taught me to bake. Do you like tea cakes?"

I swallow my surprise. "Yes."

Russian tea cakes are my favorite, not that I've had one for years.

"Do you have any powdered sugar?"

"I'll order some. What else?"

She rattles off a short list, and I order it to be delivered from the local grocery store. Forty-five minutes later, one of the soldiers knocks on the door with the ingredients.

Another thirty minutes, and my apartment is filled with the delicious scent of warm vanilla and sugar.

I wanted to tell Kira.

About her father.

I tried.

But in the end, I couldn't quite choke it out. Especially when I realized she didn't need me adding another layer of trauma to what was already a difficult day.

Now, nothing satisfies me more than seeing her make herself at home in my kitchen. It's not that I think a woman belongs in the kitchen. I didn't grow up with a mother at home. I never had that sort of ideal.

But I like the way she seems comfortable here. Like she belongs here.

When the cookies have cooled, we sit at the table and dip them into milk.

"How much older was Anya?" I ask.

"Four years. She was like a mother to me in many ways."

"Did you have a mother?"

"Our mother was a ghost of a person. She worked very hard for very little pay. Our dad was a deadbeat, so I think she was just sort of checked out emotionally. Almost like a zombie. She did help us out with Mika after he was born. Babies have a way of bringing out qualities you didn't know you had."

Her eyes fill with tears.

"Mika is well." Ravil forwarded me the photo of the teen. He is still discussing with the boy's adopted father if they even want contact with Kira. "Kira, he may not want or need your presence in his life anymore. Are you prepared for that?"

She stares at me. Her light blue eyes are wide, causing some of the water in them to spill. She sucks in a sobbing breath and holds it then lets it out slowly. "Yes," she nods. "I guess if he's happy, I'm happy. I've been so worried about him. I guess I thought he needed to be rescued."

"You were so brave to come here all by yourself to rescue him. In a foreign country, with no help. Going undercover into a bratva stronghold. Very brave."

She lets out a watery laugh. "But I screwed up completely."

I raise my brows. "Did you?"

We stare at each other across the table. I want her to feel what I do. That our explosive encounter was a gift. Something meant to be. She will get the result she desired–the information about her nephew, but she also gets this.

The intangible connection forged between the two of us.

The one I want to keep forging until it's as thick as a rope and stronger than iron.

"Didn't I?" she asks, her voice softer than feathers.

I shake my head slowly.

She gets up abruptly from her chair. Considering she's my prisoner and her hands are unfettered, I take note when she launches herself at me with vicious intent.

But it's to kiss me. To straddle my lap and sweep her tongue between my lips. She tastes of powdered sugar and sweetness.

I grip her hips and yank her over my lap, needing that warm core rubbing over my swelling cock. My hands slide up inside her sweater, cupping her breast over her bra.

She unbuttons my shirt then loses patience and tries to rip it open. When she's unsuccessful, I chuckle and do it myself, sending the buttons in a spray around us.

I yank off her sweater, unhook her bra. She removes my undershirt and works open my belt buckle, all the while moving her lips across mine in a frenzy.

I stand, picking her up with me. Her legs wrap around my waist, and we continue to kiss as I carry her to the bedroom. I lay her gently in the center of the bed and unbutton her jeans as I toe off my boots. She kicks off her boots and lifts her hips for me to pull off her jeans and panties. I shove down my jeans and step out of them. Her hands are all over me, stroking along my shoulders and up my neck, pulling me down to her. She wraps those long, lean legs around my back and uses them to draw my hips down to hers.

I grab a condom from the bedside table. She takes it from me and rips it open. We are working in perfect collaboration now. Our goals perfectly aligned. Our need for each other equally desperate. Wanting to make sure she's ready to take me, I kiss down her neck to her breast and pull one nipple into my mouth.

She's impatient, though, and she reaches from my cock. I kneel up so she can roll the condom over my erection. She pulls me to her entrance. Guides me in.

I sink into her heat like I'm coming home. Like it's

where I belong. Like nothing will ever keep me from claiming this perfect pussy as my own. Forever.

"I want you," Kira moans.

"You have me." I devour her mouth with a kiss, plunging my tongue inside to fuck her with matching thrusts.

She rocks her hips to keep time with mine, meeting me, taking me deeper, riding me on the downswing.

She is everything. Moonlight. And winter water. Snowflakes swirling in tiny eddies at the beginning of a storm. She is beauty and light and darkness and death all at once.

With each thrust I'm baptized in her energy. Her divinity. Her essence that becomes something erratic and wild.

I try to keep it, to hold it. I chase it down the path, knowing I will never fully possess it yet desperate to keep trying. To die trying.

"Kira," I choke. I'm in a state of religious ecstasy. I'm worshiping at the altar of love. Of alchemy. I need her to make me whole again. To make me anew. Someone else, worthy of holding her, of keeping her forever.

She seems to be right there with me. The way she claws my arms. The frantic cries that come from her lips. Like she needs this more than she needs her own breath or blood.

"Yes." She cries out in English then in Russian. "Da. Da-da-da-da-da. *Da!*"

There's no kink involved in this coupling. No finesse. Nothing but wild, animalistic need. A feral claiming of bodies as if we could tear past the physical and claim each other's souls.

My balls draw up tight. "I'm going to come," I warn her, unable to slow myself, unable to think past my own driving need to take care of hers.

"Yes! Come!" she urges me.

I pound in and out of her as all the blood rushes below my waist. I choke on a breath, and then I'm hurtling over the edge, into oneness. Into infinite space. That floating, bodiless, wild realm where everything and nothing exist at once.

When I return to Earth, Kira's in my arms. I'm still rocking into her, but gently now, a slow deceleration. A communion. A love-song lullaby that I want to last forever.

When it ends, neither of us says a word. I roll us to our sides, and we remain there, bodies intertwined. Hearts entangled.

Souls permanently stamped with the imprint of the other.

Chapter Fourteen

K *ira*

At bedtime, Maykl grabs two towels and tells me to follow him.

"Is there a pool? Where are we going? Do I need my boots?"

"Boots yes, but not a coat. It's a hot tub."

Hot tub. I love it.

Since our explosive sex this afternoon, things have shifted even more between us. I feel far less like his captive than his cherished lover.

Thoughts of escape still flit through my mind, but each time I dismiss them faster. I'm more and more committed to staying and letting things play out with Maykl. I still don't know what that means or looks like, but I want to find out.

We leave the apartment, trailed by the two brigadiers outside the door. We take the elevator to the top floor, then take a short flight of stairs to the rooftop.

It's freezing cold, but steam rises in a thick fog from one area of the roof.

Maykl stops when we hear female laughter.

"Who is it?" a male voice calls out.

"Maykl. Sorry, I didn't know anyone was up here."

"It's all right. We're dressed. It's a party!" the female voice calls out in English with a Russian accent.

Maykl takes my hand, pulling me closer to his side as we advance.

Through the steam, I see six figures sitting in a hot tub.

"Come on in. There's plenty of room," a redhead says.

The occupants are arranged in pairs. A blond man drapes his tattooed arm around the redhead's shoulders. Kat, the young woman from the pottery studio, sits with another tattooed man, and a small, dark-haired woman is nestled against another blond man.

Maykl kicks off his boots and strips to a pair of swim shorts. I don't have a swimsuit, but I'm not shy. I strip down to my bra and panties and follow him into the tub.

"Kira, this is Maxim and Sasha, Adrian and you already met his girlfriend, Kat, and Nikolai and Chelle."

I lift a hand in shy greeting as I immerse myself in the water. Maykl catches my waist and pulls me back against him to settle on his lap.

"I'm sorry for the loss of your sister," Maxim says, answering my question of whether these people knew anything about me. If they're angry at me for what I've done, it doesn't show. Everyone relaxes casually in the hot tub as if I'm just an ordinary woman–Maykl's new girlfriend, not the woman who planted bugs and sent their security information to the FBI.

I double check his expression, but he doesn't seem to be sneering. His comment appears genuine. Perfectly polite.

Very un-bratva-like.

"Yes, sorry for your loss," Nikolai murmurs, and the other man, Adrian, nods his agreement.

"I hate when everyone knows something I don't," Sasha complains. "But I'm sorry for your loss, too."

"Um. Yes. Thank you." What does one say in a situation like this? *I'm sorry I tried to screw you, and please don't kill me?* "Uh, thank you for letting me scatter her ashes today."

Maxim's casual position doesn't change. "It was not my call."

Okay, so he's not the *pakhan*. He seems to carry himself with that kind of authority.

"Your freedom comes at Maykl's pleasure and that of our *pakhan*."

The dark-haired woman named Chelle tenses and throws me a worried glance. Nikolai covers her ears. "Ear muffs, freckles. Nothing you need to concern yourself with."

"What's going on?" Sasha asks.

Maykl's fingers splay across my belly. It feels possessive but also protective. Like he's letting me know we're a unit.

"Nothing, sugar. It's handled. You're safe," Maxim tells her.

Sasha cocks her head. "Was I not safe?"

"You're safe," he repeats firmly. To me, he says, "Your nephew and his new family will fly out to meet you tomorrow."

My lips part in surprise. *His new family.* Wow. Maykl tried to warn me of this, but I still haven't digested it. "Fly from where?"

Maxim shakes his head. "You'll learn it all when the time comes."

I lift my gaze to study Maykl. He presses a kiss to my forehead, and I relax. It can't be horrible, whatever it is they have planned for me. It doesn't feel wrong.

Nothing about any of these people feels particularly

menacing although I know all three men are bratva. They must be dangerous criminals. Yet, seeing them with the women they obviously adore makes them completely different.

Normal, almost.

Whatever normal is.

Certainly not me.

They all seem very human. The women aren't junkies or whores. They appear to be beautiful, intelligent women who are in love with their chosen partners.

And Mika is flying out to meet me.

That may be a lie or a manipulation, but it doesn't feel like one.

"Kira said she'd like to learn to throw pots," Maykl offers.

"At you," Nikolai mutters.

Maxim smirks. A joke. These men joke with each other.

Kat smiles at me. "You should. I can teach you. Want to come down tomorrow?"

"I'd love to." I answer her immediately, even though Maykl said it was something I had to earn. I'm daring him to contradict me.

He doesn't. His fingers trace around my knee in the water.

"I'll be in the studio by noon if you want to meet me."

Now I look back at Maykl. Because the truth is, I can't go anywhere unless he lets me. There are still two guards standing behind the door to the rooftop to make sure I don't escape.

"She'll be there," he says.

Ribbons of warmth slip and slide through me, weaving a pattern around my heart. Suddenly, the effort of keeping the walls of hate I erected against the bratva up takes more

The Gatekeeper

energy than just letting them crash and crumble. I don't want to stay on guard. I want to let go and trust. These people make me feel like that's possible.

Logically, I know they are very dangerous. That my life is in their hands. And yet, I also sense that if I would just trust them, everything will come out right.

These people seem happy. Their relationships appear healthy, loving, and full of respect. I guess I want what they have. Want to be a part of whatever it is that's going on in this organization.

"I'm sorry for the trouble I caused." I seek Maxim's gaze since he seems to be the leader here. "I hope…it's been contained."

Maxim studies me for a moment then gives a single nod. "It will be handled."

Maykl squeezes my hip.

I don't ask if I'm forgiven or what will happen to me.

I'm content to ride this thing out. With both Maykl and his brothers.

Chapter Fifteen

M*aykl*
I leave two brigadiers on the door to the pottery studio after dropping Kira there then go to an all-hands bratva meeting in the basement. That's where bratva business takes place. No one but the brotherhood has access to the floor beneath the parking garage. No one else even knows it exists.

We stand in a horseshoe around Ravil and Maxim for the briefing. Dima is here and so is Pavel, another brother who moved to Los Angeles to be with his girlfriend. They both must've been summoned back to Chicago for the show-down.

Ravil addresses us. "Tonight, a branch of the Moscow bratva will attempt to infiltrate the building to kill us all and take Sasha alive. All civilians, including our women and children will all be evacuated from the building this afternoon for their safety and taken to an undisclosed location. We will take their phones and electronic devices to prevent inadvertent leaking of their whereabouts.

"I have requested assistance from the Italians–the

Tacone family–to provide for their security at the location where they will be sequestered, and they have agreed.

"This group here, including myself, will remain stationed here to take down the Moscow cell when they arrive. Wear Kevlar. I want silencers on your guns and expect you to shoot to kill. Dima has breached all of their phones, so we are privy to their conversations and plans, but even so, expect surprises." Ravil surveys the group. "Any questions?"

The group is somber, but the men present square their shoulders and put their battle masks on.

"Maxim will give you each your positions. I want you in them by six p.m. Understood?"

We all nod.

"Dismissed. Go and see Maxim. Maykl, a word."

I stay as the rest of the brigadiers file to the door where Maxim gives them their orders. Only Ravil's inner circle remains where they are: Oleg, Pavel, Dima, Nikolai, and Adrian.

Ravil addresses me without preamble. "What does Kira know?"

I shake my head. "Nothing at all. She still believes she helped the FBI. Last night, she expressed remorse over her actions."

"I heard."

Ravil's expression is impossible to read. "Keep her here tonight. She stays at your side. She's a part of this."

I tense, not liking it, but also not about to argue with my *pakhan*.

As if reading my mind, he says, "She's *politsiya*. She's accustomed to danger."

"What purpose does she serve in the fray?" I have to ask.

The Gatekeeper

"I need to see where her loyalties truly lie. She cannot remain here beyond tonight if I'm not sure."

I feel as though Ravil has a hold of my windpipe and is choking the life out of me, but it's just the thought of Kira not remaining past tonight.

I'd give anything to make that not true. To ensure I keep her forever.

But this is her test. I understand it. I may fucking hate it, but I understand it.

"Yes, *Pakhan*."

He tips his head toward the door. "Get your position from Maxim."

* * *

Kira

Something's happening.

I had a perfect day, starting with mind-blowing sex, followed by a pottery lesson and then making an early steak dinner with Maykl in his kitchen. Over dinner, he told me that Mika and his family had arrived and were checking into the Waldorf Astoria.

Now, though, he keeps looking out the window at the street below like a soldier expecting trouble.

"What's happening?" I ask. "Are the FBI coming tonight?"

He doesn't answer. But he strides to his closet and emerges with two bullet-proof vests. "Put this on." He hands me one.

"Maykl, what's happening?"

"They're coming." He pulls the vest on over his shirt and fastens it in place then pops a comms unit in his ear.

I stare at the vest he gave me, guilt ratcheting up into my

throat. I caused this. There are many innocent people in the building who could be hurt.

I try to hand it back to him. "Someone else should wear this. Give it to one of the civilians here."

He shakes his head as he screws a silencer on his pistol and then tucks it in a holster at his hip. "They are protected. Put it on, Kira. I need to know you're safe."

My stomach drops down to my feet. I caused this whole thing, and all he's worried about is my safety. I throw my arms around him in a tight embrace.

He holds me fiercely then abruptly releases me. "Put it on. We have to go soon."

I slide my arms through the heavy vest and fasten it in place. "Where are we going?"

Maykl tucks his weapon and ammo in a holster then adjusts my vest, tightening it. "To the parking garage. That's where we expect the breach."

"Breach?"

He slides a glance in my direction, and I suddenly suspect he's not being honest with me.

I narrow my eyes. "Wouldn't they come in the front doors with a warrant?" I don't know American laws that well, but I've seen their movies.

"Come." Maykl's voice is curt now. He's all business. He opens the door and tips his head toward the hallway.

"What's happening, Maykl?" I follow his swift footsteps down the hallway. Instead of taking the elevator, we take the stairwell down to the basement level but don't exit. Maykl opens the door, nods at someone, and closes it again.

"Have a seat." He indicates the steps.

I don't move.

He leans a shoulder against the wall, positioned so he can see through the narrow window of the reinforced steel door. "Maykl and Kira in position." He speaks into his comms.

"Did you really believe you were aiding the FBI, Kira?" He doesn't look at me when he speaks, just keeps looking through the window.

I go still at his question, ice cold washing over my skin. *Blyad'.*

What have I done?

I quickly review the facts. I never spoke to any American agency. All of the information was sent directly to Stepanov, who very easily could have...ugh. The realization hits me like a punch to the gut.

Of course, he's in the pocket of the bratva. Why wouldn't he be? Half the police force in Moscow is.

Gospodi, how I got played!

"Who is coming, Maykl?" I whisper, even though I already know.

"Moscow bratva."

Tears fill my eyes. "What do they want?"

"To kill everyone and take Sasha. She is the heiress of the previous *pakhan* in Moscow. The owner of oil wells that are worth many millions."

I sink to the steps and bury my face in my hands. "I'm so sorry." My voice is clogged with guilt.

Maykl looks at me for the first time since we started the conversation. "You did what you thought you had to do to find your nephew."

Tears spill. "How can you be so forgiving? I brought you a war. People will die tonight, and it's all my fault."

Maykl holds up a finger, listening to his comms device. "Copy." To me, he says in a low voice, "They're here. Simultaneous breach of the front door and the parking garage." He takes his pistol from the holster and removes the safety.

"Let's go." He turns the door handle silently and drops to a crouch as he exits.

I follow suit, staying behind him, mimicking his moves. I make sure the door closes without a sound. We creep behind one of the cars in the garage and wait. A few moments later, eight figures stride into the underground parking lot. They aren't dressed in black. They aren't stealthy. They strut in like they own the place. They divide up, four men moving to the right, four to the left.

When they each climb atop a car, I frown and glance at Maykl.

One of them reaches toward the ceiling, and I suddenly understand. "Explosives," I mouth, then simulate a bomb exploding with my hands.

Maykl's eyes blaze with purpose, and he lifts his head, aims his gun, and fires three times. "They have explosives," he barks into his comms unit between the second and third shot.

Three men drop.

Someone else fires from the opposite corner of the garage. Another silenced shot, so one of the Chicago bratva members, no doubt.

The remaining five intruders shout to each other and drop from the cars, crouching out of view. And then the garage goes dead silent.

I wish to God I had a weapon myself.

Well, fuck it. I know how to get one. I creep behind the cars, hugging the concrete wall.

Maykl reaches for me, trying to grab my arm, but I'm already too far. I move quickly toward the closest fallen body.

A bullet pings near me, shot from a silenced gun.

The Gatekeeper

Friendly fire. I hear Maykl bark something angry and urgent.

I keep moving. I'm drawing closer.

I hear the soft scrape of shoes on concrete. The rasp of breath close by. I find the body and quickly search it for a gun. As I do, I'm fired upon.

I yank the pistol up and return fire, running to duck for cover behind another car. Maykl fires from his corner to cover me.

These guns are loud; hopefully they won't draw the attention of the local police.

There's more gunfire, and I see two guys escaping onto the street. I curse under my breath and move to follow when someone fires at me.

I duck back down and point my gun around the car, adjusting the car's mirror out to show me more of the surroundings.

I catch sight of a crouched figure behind the next car. Moving as stealthily as I can, I skirt around the vehicle and raise my gun, pointing it.

"Freeze," I bark in Russian. Maykl may be comfortable shooting to kill, but my police procedure drills override that instinct in me.

"Kira."

It's Stepanov.

Fuck. I should have shot him immediately because now that I'm looking at him in the eyes, it's impossible to pull the trigger. He's my boss. Or he was.

Still, I don't lower the gun. He used me. Lied to me. Probably never planned to help me find Mika.

His brow wrinkles. "Kira?"

"Where are the FBI, Stepanov?" I demand.

"Kira!" Maykl jogs toward me, gun pointed at Stepanov.

Another man also runs from the shadows–Nikolai. "Step out of the way–I have orders to kill."

In the moment, my attention diverts to Maykl, Stepanov surges to his feet, snatches my gun, and seizes me, putting my own gun to my head. "Don't move or she dies." He wraps his forearm around my neck and yanks back, dragging me backward.

"No!" Maykl immediately stops advancing. He puts both his hands in the air.

Nikolai moves forward slowly, gun still pointed.

"Put the guns down," Stepanov shouts.

I consider fighting. But I know too well how swiftly my life would end if that trigger went off.

"She's working with him," Nikolai growls.

"No." I seek Maykl's gaze. "I'm not, I swear. I'm sorry I didn't kill him. I should have."

"Ah, I see how it is now." Stepanov sounds delighted. "This is the man you seduced? Maykl ____?" He's dragging me backward as he speaks. "I did a little research on your lover, Kira. I found something out that might interest you."

I see the look of dismay in Maykl's eyes. "No. Let her go!" He shouts in Russian. "I'm putting my gun down, you see?" He slowly lowers his hands and stoops to put his gun on the concrete floor. "Put it down!" he yells at Nikolai, who slowly does the same.

"He doesn't want me to tell you. Do you see?" Stepanov is gloating now.

My skin crawls with gooseflesh. I don't understand what it is Stepanov could possibly tell me.

"Do you want to know who killed your father, Kira? I mean which man actually pulled the trigger?"

No.

My blood freezes to ice in my veins.

No no no no no.
"What?"

There's a wild rushing in my ears. My temples throb like icepicks have been stabbed in both sides. I can barely see.

Stepanov keeps walking us both backward.

"It's...it's not true, is it?" I seek Maykl's gaze, but all I see swirling there is guilt. Regret. "Maykl?"

"Kira, I'm sorry."

"Did you know?" I practically wail the words. Stepanov has now pulled me back to the mouth of the parking garage, to street level. "This whole time? You knew you killed my father?"

"I'm sorry. Kira–he sold your sister. He tried to sell you, too, in that moment when he was begging for his life."

Stepanov takes his gun from my head and fires at Maykl, striking him in the middle of the chest.

Maykl's thrown backward, onto his back.

Knowing he's wearing Kevlar and probably survived the shot, I slam my elbow into Stepanov's ribs, grab his wrist and swing the gun up in the air before he can fire on Nikolai.

Nikolai picks up his gun from the floor and aims it at Stepanov, but at that moment, a car screeches up to the curb and a door is thrown open. Stepanov throws himself into it, and it screeches off as he slams the door.

Nikolai lifts his gun in frustration then turns to offer a hand to help a winded Maykl to his feet.

I can't move for a moment, my feet sealed to the concrete. I'm still trying to assimilate it all.

Maykl killed my father.

And he knew it this whole time.

I clutch my stomach, suddenly wanting to puke.

"Kira," Maykl croaks.

I shake my head. "Don't," I warn, but he goes on.

"I wanted to tell you. I did. I tried, do you remember?"

But I don't want to hear it. I can't. Maykl's moving toward me, but I can barely see him, my eyes are too blurred with tears.

I can't take any of this. I should have known happiness was not in the cards for me. It figures fate would deliver me to the door of my father's killer. God–if I believed there was one–must be having a great big laugh at my expense.

"Don't!" I cry, holding my palm out, as if to ward him away. "Stay back."

He stops. Spreads his hands. "Kira, please."

Tears streak down my cheeks. "No, Maykl. Just...no. I can't. I...have to go."

I turn and run out onto the street. I don't even know where I'm going or what I'll do. I don't have any of my things with me. No money or passport. All I can think is that I need to get away from Maykl.

"Kira–wait! Kira!" Maykl calls after me, but I'm running fast and hard, slipping on the icy sidewalks and then catching my stride again, doing everything I can to just get away.

Chapter Sixteen

Maykl

Nikolai grabs my arm. "Let her go."

I shake him off, even though moving pains my bruised ribs. "Kira!" I run out to the street in time to see Kira racing away toward the lake.

I start after her, but Nikolai calls after me. "Respect her wishes. Give her space."

That stops me. I don't want to disrespect Kira. I've already done plenty of that, starting with not telling her I killed her father.

Blyad'.

It guts me to stand and watch her go, though. Absolutely ruins me.

"Come. We need to check the bombs," Nikolai reminds me.

Double-fuck.

He's right. They were planting bombs to bring our entire building down.

I shudder to think what would've happened if we hadn't known they were coming.

But no, we still would have caught them. They were clumsy and disorganized and had far too few men to actually take us down.

Dima is already examining one of the bombs. "It wasn't armed yet," he reports.

Nikolai goes to the other one, and I carefully pick up the third to bring to Dima for inspection, since explosives aren't my area of expertise.

I hear the chatter on the comms. It sounds like the team who entered upstairs was quickly eliminated, as was the team who attempted to breach our air intake to pump in poisoned gas. Kuznets isn't among any of the men killed.

Nikolai reports that three men got away, including Stepanov. He leaves out Kira also walking out.

I don't know if she was still considered our prisoner, but it doesn't matter. She proved her loyalty as far as I'm concerned. She disarmed Stepanov before he shot at Nikolai. And if Ravil wants to slit my throat for letting her walk, I'll offer it to him.

At this point, I'd almost prefer that fate to the terrible ripping sensation in my chest. The feeling of having my heart rent from my chest and dragged flopping behind me on a chain.

And it isn't from the bullet bruising my ribs.

Heartache doesn't begin to describe the desolation crashing through me.

I walk through the parking garage and up the stairs.

I pass the first floor where I should go to report to Ravil. I keep walking up flight after flight. Passing my own floor.

Passing the next one and the next.

I walk up all forty flights of stairs until I get to the rooftop.

Only when I arrive out on the rooftop do I realize why I

came here. I go to the railing and stand to look over the edge.

I'm looking for Kira.

Trying to figure out where she might have gone.

She had no jacket. No money. No passport. She'll have to come back.

Except I know, as soon as I think it, that she won't.

Kira is a warrior. She's stubborn and strong. She will not slink back here to collect her things. No, the only way she'd come back would be with the FBI or police to arrest me for kidnapping and murder.

I search the sidewalks below, trace the lake shore for her slim figure or pale blonde hair, but of course, it's dark. I can't make out anyone down there.

Damn it.

"Where in the fuck is Maykl?" I hear Ravil demand in the comms unit.

"Coming." I move for the door.

"In the basement," Ravil instructs. "Where's the girl?"

"I let her go." Heaviness soaks the words. Like I just dropped an anchor into the depths of the sea and will never be able to move from the spot in my life again.

Ravil may kill me over this. Fuck. He may kill Kira over this. That I can't allow. I jog into the elevator to take it down to the first floor.

But Nikolai speaks. "Kira may not be a problem. She ran because her boss dropped the bomb that Maykl pulled the trigger on her father."

Ravil curses. "Is that true?"

"Yes, *Pakhan*."

"And you knew that?"

The elevator plunges down. "I tried to tell her. I wanted to. But I also didn't want to fuck things up."

"It's me you should have told," Ravil growls.

I stab my fingers through my hair. "I know. I guess I was hoping...it wouldn't come to light. He was my initiation kill. I was thirteen." I slump against the side of the elevator then, purposely smacking my head into the wall just to feel something other than the anguish choking me. "I never knew Fate would bring me the one woman who wants me dead."

The elevator doors open, and I step out into the scene. The bratva members quickly work to move bloody bodies onto laundry carts to be wheeled out the secret exit. The exit we used to get all the occupants out safely this afternoon.

Adrian looks at me as he drags a body out from the other elevator. Great. The entire inner circle has been privy to my fuck-up via the comms. "Maybe Fate brought her to you to make things right."

I remember that Adrian kidnapped Kateryna because her father was responsible for enslaving Adrian's sister, Nadia. What started out as a revenge mission turned into love.

But that was different. It wasn't Kat who had done the harm to Adrian, it was her father.

I took Kira's father, and there's nothing I can say or do to make up for that.

I pull my comms unit out of my ear.

"So what happened?" Ravil demands. He and Maxim stand together giving orders.

I don't have the energy to explain. Not even knowing Ravil may punish or kill me. Nikolai comes up beside me and recounts the entire scene to them.

"So we have Kuznets, Stepanov, and two soldiers still at large," Maxim says.

"*If* Kuznets even came. He may have just sent Stepanov

The Gatekeeper

to do the dirty work. Then he'll claim he knew nothing about it," Ravil says.

"The phones I hacked have been discarded," Dima reports.

Ravil curses. "Do we think Kira will make contact with them?"

I shake my head. "No. She was on our side before..."

"Her motivation is the nephew," Maxim reminds us, and a streak of relief runs through me as I realize I know exactly where she is right now.

"I told her where they were staying," I say.

"That's where she'll go." Ravil pulls out his phone.

I must have a death wish because I reach for it. Maxim shoves me back. "Let her go," I say gruffly. "She's not a threat."

"That's for us to assess," Maxim reminds me.

"Offer her help, then," I plead. "She has nothing with her–no phone or money, nor her passport. If we don't want her to call Stepanov for assistance, we need to step in."

"Oh, but I do want her to call Stepanov for assistance." Ravil holds the phone to his ear. "How else will I kill the *mudak*?"

"Go and get her things," Maxim says. "We'll deliver them to the hotel for her."

"After Dima installs trackers," Ravil says.

"She won't go to him." I don't know whether it's true, or I just want it to be true. She may go running straight to her boss, considering what she now thinks of me.

Maxim points to the elevator. "Move, Maykl."

I don't, though. I'm having a hard time just remembering how to stand on my two feet. How to keep my heart beating. How to breathe.

Nothing feels natural anymore with Kira lost to me.

Dima comes to my side and takes my arm. "Come on. I'll go with you to put the trackers in."

* * *

Kira

I don't realize how cold I am. The heat of betrayal propels me forward, along the lake, one foot in front of the other.

I can't believe Maykl killed my father. Every horrible moment in my life has been wrought by the bratva. And the moment I start to think I can get past it, that I might actually be able to forgive and move on, I discover the man I was falling for murdered my father.

It's just...too much to take.

I can't even absorb the information. That's why I ran.

Honestly, I don't want to absorb it. I don't want to think about it ever again. I just want to get the hell away from everything to do with the bratva.

Eventually, though, I stop and turn around. I've come a couple of miles, at least.

I don't know where to go. What to do.

I turn out to face the lake, drawn to it. I walk down the sand beach to the shore. My tears are frozen to my cheeks. My fingers numb icicles.

I realize why I'm standing here. Because Anya's out there. Her essence is cradled in that water.

"What would you do?" I whisper then instantly regret it. I know what Anya would do. Find a hit to numb her pain.

That's when I remember Mika.

That he's here to see me. In a hotel somewhere.

Blyad', I have no money or phone to even take a bus anywhere. I walk back to the sidewalk.

"Excuse me?" I stop a couple on the street.

The woman gives me a frightened look. I'm sure I look strange in this Kevlar vest, with no jacket. My cheeks are probably bright pink, chapped from the wind.

"Do you have any idea where the Waldorf Astoria hotel is?"

The woman's face clears. She points behind her. "It's on the corner right there. At the end of this block, see the sign?"

It's the first time anything has gone right for me on this trip.

"Yes, thank you."

I shove the pain spearing my heart out of my awareness and just focus on Mika. I saw his photo. I know he's alive. Hopefully the fact that he's here wasn't a lie.

The doorman holds the door open for me, and the warm air shocks my frozen skin. The lights are a glare to my eyes.

It's late, so hardly anyone is around. I don't even know who to ask for at the front desk. I could try Mika's name, but I doubt it will work.

But then a man gets up from the bar and comes toward me. I don't know him, but he must be bratva–I see the tattoos that creep above the collar of his expensive shirt. Plus, he's carrying my purse and suitcase.

I stand in the middle of the beautiful lobby, trembling. Waiting for him to come to me.

"Kira?"

I nod.

"You look like him." He tips his head. "And her."

So he knew Anya.

Tears fill my eyes. "Are you–?

The man holds out a hand. "My name is Vlad. I'm Mika's adopted father."

"Oh." Tears spill down my cheeks.

He holds out the suitcase and my purse. "Maykl brought your things by for you. And he wanted me to give you this." He takes a thick envelope from inside his jacket pocket and hands it to me. The flap is open, and inside I see a stack of one hundred dollar bills. "For your hotel expenses."

"Where's—"

"You can see Mika in the morning. Let's get you checked in." He picks up my suitcase again.

The man is unbelievably kind. Another bratva man who doesn't fit the image in my mind. And Maykl brought my things...

I barely keep from dropping to my knees and crying like a baby.

Somehow, I follow Vlad to the reception desk and provide my passport and a credit card to get checked in.

Vlad carries my suitcase to the elevator and gets in it with me.

I marshal my thoughts. "What happened to Anya here? Why is Mika with you?"

Vlad's lips thin into a line. "Anya abandoned Mika with us not long after she moved here." He tips his head. "She had a nasty drug habit."

The old me would've lashed back that it was the bratva's fault, but I don't have any fight left in me. Nothing is black or white anymore. Good or bad.

The elevator stops on my floor, and we get out. Vlad goes on. "Honestly, I considered Mika to be Aleksi's problem since he's the one who brought them out with us. But..." He draws a breath. "I was called back to Russia for personal matters, and while I was away, the men in my cell—including Aleksi—were massacred by the Italian mafia.

The Gatekeeper

When I returned, I found Mika had been living on his own in our house for weeks. He'd been stealing food and wallets from the streets to get by. I took him back to Russia, but he did not wish to contact his family. He did go and look in the window at his grandmother once but decided against making contact."

Tears spill from my eyes. "Yes...my mother wasn't much to him. She wasn't much to anybody. I can see that."

"He stayed with me in Volgograd, and after I moved to Las Vegas to marry, my wife and I legally adopted him. My wife is a teacher. She tutored him up, and now he's in high school. Straight A's. He's a very smart kid." Vlad says it proudly and fresh tears streak my cheeks. "He's not interested in sports, but he's strong. He boxes at a gym." Vlad shrugs. "Grew up with violence." He says it matter-of-factly.

Once more, I can't find it in me to rail against that violence. Not when it seems Mika found people who love and care for him.

We stop in front of my door.

"Thank you," I say. "I...look forward to seeing him in the morning."

"We're in suite 399. Come at ten."

I still, suddenly wondering if it's safe for me. But of course, if Maykl's cell wanted me back, they would have grabbed me downstairs.

"It's not a trap," Vlad says as if reading my mind. "Although if you know where to find your boss, there are some people who want him dead." He doesn't wait for my reply, he just strides off in his tailored slacks and shined shoes, his gait both graceful and lethal–like a lion in his jungle.

I open the hotel door and go inside. My skin burns from

the cold. My head aches. I'm parched from so much crying. I should take a shower, but I can't put the effort in. Instead, I fall face down on the bed and don't move until morning.

* * *

Maykl

I stay out of my apartment, sitting downstairs at the front desk all night. I'm not watching the door for her.

I know she won't be back.

Especially not when I brought her things to her and made it easy for her to go home.

Ravil hasn't green-lighted the return of the civilians to the building yet, so it's dead quiet. Of course, it's always dead quiet at this time of night.

The lobby suffered a few bullet holes, but the blood's been scrubbed from the floors and the bodies disposed of. My biggest failure as a gatekeeper. I couldn't keep Kira out of the building, nor out of my heart.

It's a wonder I'm still breathing. I still don't know what Ravil might have in store for me.

I text Kira. *I know there's nothing I can do to give you back your father. I'm sorry for the pain I caused you and your family. If you ever need anything, I will provide it.*

I don't expect her to answer. I'm not dumb enough to believe she will. But I want her to have my number, just the same. I would do almost anything for her if she asked me to–swallow nails. Jump off a cliff.

Dima gave me access to the app he uses to monitor her trackers, so I know she hasn't moved from her hotel room since Vlad texted me that she checked in.

I don't sleep. I'm not trying to stay awake, either, but no part of me wants to close my eyes.

The Gatekeeper

Every time I do, I see Kira's face when Stepanov told her. The way she looked at me–the pain of my betrayal evident in the horror in her eyes.

I spend the night going over and over what I could have done differently. What I could do to ease the trauma I inflicted, but I come up with nothing.

What's done is done. I don't know how to fix it.

But I also don't know how to go on. She was only here a few short days, but in that time, she left an indelible mark on me. I'm forever changed by knowing her. By tasting her. By seeing her cry.

I don't see how I can make it through another day knowing how badly I hurt her. Only God knows that I never meant to.

Chapter Seventeen

Kira

Even though I tried to block all thoughts of Maykl, I wake replaying the moment in which he told me about killing my father.

Because I realize, he did try to tell me. He told me everything but who the man he killed was. I know that he didn't want to do it. He felt he had no choice. That he was only thirteen–the same age I was at the time. I'm guessing, like me, he probably didn't even know why it happened.

I crawl off the bed steeped in sorrow.

But the sorrow isn't just for me.

It's also for Maykl.

And for us.

The loss of us. Because what we had was special. Remarkable, even. I don't trust people. Haven't let a single man into my heart since the day the bratva took Anya. I've avoided intimacy. Rejected closeness, seeing it as weakness.

But somehow, unbelievably, I came to trust Maykl–the last man on Earth I should have let my guard down with.

He captured me and held me prisoner and still somehow made me fall in love.

I check my phone and find he messaged me. Like a fool, I hold the phone to my chest.

I don't answer, though. I'm still too battered by it all to even function. And right now, I need to get myself showered and dressed to see Mika.

The Waldorf is a beautiful hotel, not that Maykl's apartment wasn't just as luxurious. I turn on the shower and step under the spray of water, washing off the horror of yesterday.

Flashes of the damage I caused keep splintering through my thoughts. The siege on the Kremlin. The shoot-out in the garage. *Gospodi*, what if the Moscow bratva had succeeded in their plan to kidnap Sasha? It would have been all my fault. How could I have been so stupid?

Did I really think I was working for the FBI? What an idiot. I can only chalk it up to my grief and fear over Mika's well-being.

Stepanov used me. Put a gun to my head, the bastard!

I shove the thoughts away. First, I see Mika.

Then I can figure the rest of this out.

I get dressed and go down to the lobby for coffee and a muffin. My stomach is in knots and my mouth is dry. I barely choke down the breakfast then go to Vlad's hotel suite and knock on the door.

An American woman answers the door with a smile. "Hi. Kira? I'm Alessia, Mika's adopted mom." An adorable blonde preschooler hugs her leg. "This is our daughter, Lara."

They have more than one child. Like a real family. For some reason, that warms my heart.

"Come on in." She holds the hotel door open for me,

and I step in, looking past her and the child to take in the teenager behind her. He stands nearly six feet tall. He's lean and lanky like he just had a growth spurt. He stands beside Vlad, imitating his adopted father's watchful stance.

"Mika."

"Hey." He sounds like an American, too. A gruff, awkward, normal American teenager. My heart squeezes.

"Do you remember me?" I speak in Russian.

He answers in English. "Yeah. Sort of. A little bit."

I'm not usually a hugger, but I go in for an embrace.

He returns it, awkwardly.

"I'm sorry I didn't come for you sooner. Your mom and I–we had a fight about her coming to America. I didn't want her to leave. I begged her to leave you with me, but she wouldn't hear of it. And because of our fight, she stopped speaking to me. I lost touch with her. I didn't know anything until I was contacted by the consulate last week–" I stop, abruptly, and catch Vlad's gaze. "Does he know?"

"That Anya's dead?" Mika asks bitterly. "Yeah."

My eyes flood. "I'm so sorry she left you. I wish I'd known, Mika. I swear I would have come to get you."

He takes a step back, and I make an effort to rein in my emotions.

"I'm sorry," I say again.

"It's fine." He's back to awkward. "You're not taking me back to Russia, though."

"No." I glance at Vlad and Alessia. "You have a new family now. I'm so glad."

Lara, the little girl, taps my leg to show me a children's book. The lettering is Cyrillic. I smile at her. "Do you speak Russian?" I ask in my native tongue.

"I can read this," she boasts, answering in Russian.

Mika rolls his eyes. "She has it memorized. She doesn't

read yet." He beckons to Lara, who brings him the book. He cracks it open and points at an elephant. "Who's that?"

Oh God. It's so normal and absolutely precious. Mika has a mom and a dad and a little sister, and they are storybook sweet. I thought I would need to swoop in and rescue him, but he's flourishing here.

"We'll be here all week," Alessia says. "I'm from Chicago, and half my family lives here. I thought we could maybe show you around the city, so you can spend some time with Mika. We could take the kids to Shedd Aquarium this afternoon," Alessia says. "I was going to see if my sister-in-law and her two kids wanted to come, too."

I bob my head. "Yes. Absolutely. I'd love to." I blink rapidly to hold back my tears. I don't want to make Mika uncomfortable. "That is so kind of you."

And then I realize I can't.

Not while my stomach is in knots and my heart is torn in two.

Now that I know and have seen with my own eyes how happy and adjusted Mika is, I need to fix everything that's broken with me.

Starting with Maykl and possibly ending with Stepanov.

"There are some things I need to take care of, first."

Vlad nods like he knows what happened yesterday. He probably does since he was waiting for me to show up last night.

"May I get your cell number and be in touch as soon as I can join you?"

"Absolutely. Give me your phone." Alessia has that easy manner of being warm and familiar with me, even though we're strangers. Like Sasha and Kat were with me.

I haven't had many friends–female or male. Most of my

life was about surviving my family situation. Anya was my best friend until she wasn't, and I never really recovered from losing her.

I hand her my phone, and she enters her number and returns it with a smile.

"Great. Thanks. I, um…I need to go, but I look forward to spending time with you later."

Mika lifts his hand in an awkward farewell.

I wave back. "Thank you both," I say to Vlad and Alessia. "For flying out here and meeting me. It means so much."

"Go on," Vlad says. "We'll see you again soon."

I'm already backing toward the door. "Yes. Thank you."

I practically run for the elevator. Now that I have a purpose, now that I've figured out what needs to be done, I can't wait another second.

I take the elevator downstairs, and the doorman hails me a cab for the short drive to the Kremlin.

I rush through the front doors, hoping to see Maykl behind the desk, but he's not there. There's an armed guard stationed just inside the door. Behind the desk, an older man surveys me with narrowed eyes.

"I'm here to see Maykl," I say to him in Russian. "Can you tell him Kira is here?"

"I know who you are." There's accusation in his gaze, which I fully deserve. "Maykl is with our *pakhan*. Answering for letting you go free, no doubt."

I square my shoulders and lift my chin. "Tell your *pakhan* I'm here to surrender. I want to help get Stepanov. I should have killed him yesterday."

The old man picks up his cell phone and texts something. A moment later, he beckons the guard near the door. "Take her to Ravil."

I follow the guard into the elevator to the top floor, where a giant man awaits. He doesn't speak but beckons me to follow him into a gorgeous penthouse suite and down a hallway to an office.

Inside, a blond man sits behind a desk. He's younger than I expected, perhaps in his early forties. Maxim sits in a chair opposite the desk, and he pulls out a seat for me.

"Where's Maykl?" I ask, suddenly afraid for him.

Did he suffer some kind of punishment for letting me go? If so, I will never forgive myself.

"Sit." Ravil has mastered the art of imperiousness.

I work to calm my racing pulse as I sink into the chair beside Maxim. I'm still in my woolen coat because it doesn't feel right to take it off. I don't know how long I'm staying. Or if I'm welcome to get comfortable.

I drop into the seat and wait for him to say something, but he just studies me, so I speak. "I want to help you catch Stepanov."

"Oh, I won't be catching him," Ravil says. "I'll be killing him."

I ignore the goosebumps racing across my arms. Making the hairs at the back of my neck stand.

I don't condone murder. That's why I couldn't shoot at Stepanov when I had the chance. But I don't feel particularly judgmental over his desire to end the man who tried to kill him and blow up his building.

If they hadn't had advance warning, every occupant of this building might be dead right now.

"I can call him and ask for help. If they're not watching the building, they may not know which side I'm on."

"Why would you do this thing?" Ravil asks. There's nothing friendly about his visage. His expression is stony, his gaze cold.

I clasp my trembling hands together. "Because it's my fault they got in. I caused this problem for you, and I want to fix it."

"You are working with the real FBI now, perhaps?"

Of course, he mistrusts me. What reason have I given for them to take my word?

I shake my head. "No. I'm...I'm with you. I mean–" *Gospodi,* what do I mean? I swallow and try to swallow the lump in my throat. "My loyalties are here with–"

"With whom?"

"With Maykl." My eyes fill with tears. "Where is he? Did you... is he safe?"

Ravil appears satisfied. "He is safe," he assures me.

He tips his head at Maxim. "Bring him in."

I stand from my chair, my breath caught up in my throat. A moment later, Maxim returns with Maykl. I run to him as if our one night apart had been a million years.

It felt even longer. I now know what it would be like to live without him, and I know I never want that.

I don't want to go back to Russia. I don't want to return to my old, hollow life. I don't care about any of it.

All I know is that Maykl somehow repaired the things in me that were broken. And yes, he was responsible for one of those wounds, but I know he'd do anything he could to make it up to me. And, ultimately, as much as I love my dad, he caused his own demise. And he sold Anya.

I fly into Maykl, and he wraps his arms around me, holding me tight.

"Moya malen'kaya Valkiriya," he murmurs.

"Fix things with her," Ravil says to Maykl. "Then we move on Stepanov. Go."

* * *

Maykl

I can't believe it. Kira is here. In my arms.

She still wants me.

I bustle her out of the penthouse, in a hurry to get her somewhere private. I opt for the stairs to the roof, since she's wearing her red coat. Taking her hand, I lead her up to the roof's edge where I cradle her face in my hands.

"I'm sorry, Kira. I'm sorry I was the one. I wish it was different. I wish I knew how to make it up to you."

She holds my wrists. "I'm okay. I...I can't even say I'm sorry it happened. Because if you hadn't been the one, you never would've been in the bratva, and then... someone else would've been guarding that door the night arrived."

My eyes burn.

"Sweet *Valkiriya*. We would have met. If not here, there. Somehow. We were destined for each other."

"Yes." Her laugh is watery. "Yes, we would have met."

"So..." I don't know how to ask this. "Are you...Will you stay? I want you, Kira. I don't want to let you go home. Or leave this building. Or my life. Please... tell me you'll stay."

She nods. "I'm staying. I have nothing to go back to. Mika is here in the States. My job was bogus. My boss is a criminal. My life was empty before I met you. That's a fact."

I kiss her, claiming her soft lips. She moves them against mine with a whimper. I catch the back of her head to hold her in place, deepen the kiss. We slow dance as we kiss, rocking from foot to foot, slowly circling each other as we come apart and go back in, each time a different tempo. Soft and meaningful, then intense with passion, then a slow savoring.

"I love you." She says it first, and it feels like my life

both ends and begins at once. Like if I dived from this building, I could fly.

"I love you, little warrior."

She lifts those ice-blue eyes, and they crinkle at the corners.

"How was your nephew?"

She smiles and nods. "He's good. All grown up. He seems happy with Vlad and Alessia. Really happy. It's a much better life than Anya could have given him. I can't forgive her for abandoning him, but maybe it worked out for the best."

"Like us," I say softly.

"Yes." She wraps her arms around my middle. Like us." Then she propels me toward the door. "Come on. You don't have a jacket, and it's cold out here."

"Yes. And Ravil is waiting for us."

* * *

Kira

Maykl hates the idea of me being bait, but I can take care of myself. I have a gun strapped to my leg. According to Dima, the Chicago Bratva's hacker, Stepanov has not left the country. His phone seems to have been destroyed, though. I called the office line at work and left him a message, saying I needed help getting home because my passport and things were still at the Kremlin.

Stepanov called back and asked where I was. I told him I was staying at the flophouse where my sister's body had been found.

It seemed like something he might believe, and I sort of enjoyed the full circle of returning to the place where it all began in Chicago.

I wait now on the broken steps to the graffitied house.

A black town car pulls up. The doors don't open. No one gets out. Which means the bratva members hiding in the building to shoot, won't be able to.

I get up and walk to it, pulling open the door.

I sense Maykl's silent protest from behind the boarded-up windows of the flophouse. The Chicago bratva are waiting there, hoping to make clean kills here in a neighborhood where no one talks about criminal activities.

It's all right, though. I'm strapped with a weapon, wired for audio, and have a half-dozen trackers on me. I know Maykl and his brothers will be right behind us.

I climb into the backseat of the car, which takes off driving before I've even shut the door. "Thank you for coming to get me."

Stepanov is in the backseat. He pats me down for a weapon but misses the gun in my boot.

"I slept here last night. I ran after you left last night." I make my face sullen and stubborn. "I'm not going back."

"No? What of your lover? You won't forgive him?"

I'm not much of an actress, but I draw on the genuine anger I felt last night. The shock and betrayal that had rocked me. "Never."

But I fold my arms across my chest. "You told me I was working with the FBI."

"A little lie to ensure your cooperation," Stepanov says. "But I do have contacts there, and they are working on finding your nephew."

Another lie, I'm sure.

"But we are leaving the country right now. If you wish to come with us, this is your only chance."

"But I told you, I don't have a passport."

"You don't need one. We travel on private aircraft."

The Gatekeeper

I pretend to relax. "Good." Hopefully, Maykl heard that and knows where to go. I'm not sure I actually believe I will end up on that plane alive. Even if Stepanov's intentions are good, I don't plan on going back to Russia with them.

I sweat through the remainder of the drive. No one makes conversation, which makes it even more tense.

Seventy minutes later we reach a private airstrip where crates are being loaded onto a plane.

Stepanov gets out without a word. I follow him.

A large man with an oversized forehead stands in front of the plane, and I draw in a surprised breath. "Leonid Kuznetsov." I say it out loud, so the Chicago bratva will hear. I recognize the head of the largest branch of the Moscow bratva.

He glares at me. "Why is she here?"

"She cannot forgive her lover for what he's done. She's coming back to Russia with us." Stepanov puts a meaty hand on my nape and when his thumb slides up and down, my stomach turns. I remember how he made a play for me in the past.

I imagine he expects me to play nice with him now. Disgusting pig.

"She's your responsibility," Kuznets says.

"Of course." Stepanov maneuvers me toward the plane's entrance.

I start to panic. What if the guys don't get here in time? Do I just cut my losses and run? I have a weapon, but there's no way I can take down four men by myself. Besides, I'm not the one with a vendetta. I don't need these men dead.

I just needed to do this for Maykl. To prove my loyalty and clear my name with his brotherhood. So, I can be accepted into their circle.

"I have to use the restroom," I say, trying to avoid getting on the plane.

"Use the one in there." Stepanov jerks his thumb toward the cabin.

Blyad'.

I climb the steps to get on the plane and find the tiny bathroom where I lock myself inside to formulate a plan.

* * *

Maykl

"Where's their location?" I shout, taking a turn at fifty miles an hour. "I lost the signal." I'm in my Ford Bronco with Adrian and Dima. Two other vehicles loaded with Chicago bratva soldiers hurtle behind us.

I'm doing my best to stay calm. To keep my head in the game. Because I have to find my girl before something terrible happens to her. I don't trust Stepanov not to kill her the moment he's in a place he can dispose a body. And out here in this sparsely populated industrial area, it would be very easy to dig a grave or bury someone in concrete.

"They must have a signal jammer," Dima grumbles, swiping across his iPad. "I've got nothing. I lost all GPS information."

Adrian points across me. "I see a runway. Must be a private airstrip over there."

I slam on the brakes, causing Oleg to swerve to the right behind me to avoid a collision.

Spinning the steering wheel, I adjust my direction and peel out to the left, in the direction Adrian pointed, then I step on the gas. I get the Ford Bronco up to 90 mph, only slowing when Adrian points to the right.

I swing around a curve, and we zoom in to an industrial

The Gatekeeper

warehouse area where there's a hangar. A small plane stands on a runway. Around it men move quickly, packing crates into the cargo area.

When one of them draws a gun and fires at us, I know we found the right place. I throw the car into park as all three of us duck our heads to avoid being shot. We tumble out the doors crouched, guns drawn. I fire around my door and take out two men.

The other two vehicles slam into formation around us, forming a barricade of sorts. The cars are all bulletproof.

Gunfire rains from both sides. Bodies drop. None from our side.

I'm scanning the area for Kira, terrified she'll get caught in the fire. Of course, she knows how to handle herself. She would know to stay down. Or, use her own weapon, if it wasn't taken from her.

I don't wait for the gunfire to stop. I run, away from the safety of the vehicles, toward the airplane. I'm praying the whole time I will find Kira inside. Alive. *Gospodi,* please let her be alive.

"Kuznets is mine," I hear Ravil growl. He must have sighted him.

I still don't see Kira anywhere. I dash behind a crate to crouch, then run for the stairs to the airplane just as a shot is fired inside.

Fuck, no. *Kira!*

But, of course, my little warrior is not playing the victim. Her gun is held expertly in both hands, arms straight out, a look of determination blazing in those sky-blue eyes. At her feet lies Stepanov, a neat bullet hole in the center of his forehead.

"Kira!" I hold out my hand to help her step over her boss' body.

"Are they–"

I stop to listen. There's no gunfire. In my comms, Ravil is barking orders like we've won the battle.

"It's over," I confirm, pulling her roughly into my arms.

Thank fuck she's all right. Unharmed. Back where she's supposed to be: with me.

There will be much to do. Adrian has his job as cleaner cut out for him for the second time in two days. But I need to get Kira out of here.

"Permission to take Kira back?" I ask into the comms.

"Granted. Is she all right?" Ravil asks.

"She's safe. She killed Stepanov," I tell him, so he never questions her loyalty again.

"Good. Take care of your woman," Ravil says.

I cup the side of Kira's face and stroke my thumb over her soft skin. "I intend to."

She rises to her tiptoes to press a firm victory kiss against my lips.

I remove the comms unit from my ear and turn it off. "Come on, my beautiful Valkyrie. I need to get you out of here. I nearly died thinking of the things they might do to you." I take her hand and hurry her off the plane and into my Bronco still running on the tarmac.

I climb in beside her. The moment we're alone together, I'm satisfied.

Kira looks over and laughs.

I smile back. "What is it?"

"Nothing. Just...lightness. For the first time in my life, I have this feeling that everything is all right."

A sense of victory pumps through me, knowing that I'm a part of that lightness.

"Mika's safe and happy. My sister is...well, she's gone to

rest, if you believe that's how death works. And the Chicago bratva have won their battle."

"Is that all?" I arch a brow.

Her smile widens. "No, that's not all. There's you."

"What about me?" I prompt.

"You're mine."

I pull away, desperate to get her home and underneath me. "So, you're keeping me?"

"Well, technically, I was hoping you'd keep me. You see, I don't have a job here or anything."

I let out a soft chuckle of satisfaction. She's staying. With me.

She's mine to keep.

"*Valkiriya*, I'm never letting you go." I reach out to catch her hand and hold it. "From the first moment I got you in my apartment, I was figuring out a way to keep you there forever."

"You won't even have to use duct tape or zip ties anymore."

"I may not have to, but I probably still will."

"Promise?"

Chapter Eighteen

Kira

Maykl reaches for me the moment we step inside his apartment, pulling off my sweater, unhooking my bra. I unbutton his pants and drop to my knees.

His hands tangle in my hair. "Ah, here we are again. Full circle."

"Uh-huh." I free his erection.

"Tell me I'm the only man you've seduced that way." Maykl's touch turns possessive, his fingers tugging me forward as I take him into my mouth.

"Mmm hmm," I say around his cock.

"Fuck. You look so hot like that. But I need to hear it. Tell me, clearly, Kira." He pulls my hair to tug me off. "Am I the only one?"

"My first and only. But I think you somehow knew that?"

He relaxes and slides his dick back into my mouth. "Yes. You were nervous. An intoxicating mixture of bold and innocent."

I answer him with a long slow suck from root to tip.

He groans, a small shudder of pleasure making his legs vibrate. "I knew you were trouble, but I couldn't help myself," he confesses, his touch alternating between caresses and aggressive tugs and pulls.

I swirl my tongue on the underside of his cock as I suck, my head bobbing, my hand squeezing at the base.

I work hard to please him. Make this my apology for everything I did.

"You're so beautiful. Fuck." He pulls me off. "I need to be inside you." He grasps my forearms and lifts me to my feet, then backs me against the arm of his sofa. His fingers work frantically to open my jeans and shove them down with my panties.

I kick them off my legs, along with my shoes as he toes off his boots and kicks out of his. He lifts one of my knees to his hip and lines his cock up with my entrance. He's not wearing a condom.

"Are you clean?" I ask.

He nods.

"Me, too."

"Good, because I need to ride bareback," he growls. "Tell me you're not on birth control." He's shoving into me.

"I-I'm not," I pant. It feels so glorious to be filled by him. So satisfying. Like this is exactly what I've been missing my entire life. "Why?"

"Because I want to put my babies into you." He thrusts in and out, nailing me against the couch, getting deeper than I could have imagined possible.

"What?" I laugh, warm bubbles of pleasure fizzing and bursting their way up my middle to my chest.

"You heard me." He pumps his hips against mine. "I'm

claiming you fully, *Valkiriya*. I'm going to fill you with my cum until you're swollen and ripe with my child, and even then I'm never going to give you a break."

I don't know if I'm orgasming or laughing. I guess both. My core tightens around his glorious cock as my belly shakes, and the most perfect sounds of happiness come from my throat.

"Do you want that, Kira?" he asks.

As always, he's still attentive. Checking in to see how his vow landed. If I'm on board.

I think of Mika, so happy with his new parents. He and their sweet baby girl growing up in that circle of love.

I never had that kind of family or love. I know now that while I may have thought my dad was a decent father, I was wrong. He sold Anya. Tried to sell me. Maykl probably did the world a favor ending his life.

But Maykl? He'd be an amazing father. And I would do so much better than Anya. I would give my everything to a child.

Then, I'm laugh-crying. "*Da*," I affirm. "Yes. Let's make a family."

Maykl turns fierce, a storm of lust unleashed. He wraps an arm behind my back and pounds into me, knocking the sofa backward with each brutal thrust.

I quiver. Shake. Cry out. I'm lost in his rhythm. In these waves of passion that carry us both away.

And then we come together. Bolts of lightning must strike simultaneously around the city. Surely the earth rumbled and cracked somewhere. The gods stopped their chatter in heaven to listen and then applaud.

I light up as if electrified, squeezing and convulsing against his bucking body.

And then I go limp. Boneless. A ragdoll.

Maykl pulls out and lifts me into his arms, dropping onto the sofa and arranging me over his body, his hands on my ass, his lips on my hair.

"*Ya lyublyu tebya*," he murmurs.

"I love you, too."

Epilogue

M*aykl*

We're on a yacht on Lake Michigan. I'm in a tux, like all my brothers, waiting on the deck.

It's a beautiful June morning, the breeze blowing across the water keeping us cool enough, so we don't sweat in our monkey suits.

Benjamin, Ravil and Lucy's toddler, runs back and forth along the railing, making Lucy nervous, but looking adorable in his own tiny tuxedo. He's the ring-bearer.

Oleg looks the most uncomfortable in his, like at any moment he might pull an Incredible Hulk and bust his huge muscles through the fabric.

Flynn looks the most at ease in his tux. Dapper, even. His electric guitar is plugged into an amp, and he's playing some beautiful Spanish guitar melody. He's not Russian, nor technically a bratva brother, but he has an honorary place with us. He killed for Nadia, Adrian's sister, so he was given the ink on his skin to mark the crime.

He's not the only outsider on the yacht. A small crowd

of guests has arrived and taken seats on the top deck where the ceremony is to take place.

The captain of the ship arrives on our deck and gives us a nod, and Flynn finds an ending to his song and sets the guitar down for later. He and his sister and their bandmates will be the entertainment after the wedding.

The bratva men file out in a line. Ravil and Maxim lead the way, then Oleg and Dima, Adrian and Pavel, Flynn and me. Nikolai takes up the rear.

We wait at the top of the stairs for the music to cue us, then Ravil offers an arm to escort Lucy down the aisle, followed by Maxim and Sasha, then Oleg and a pregnant Story, Dima and Natasha, Pavel and Kayla, Adrian and Kat, Flynn and Nadia.

My gaze goes soft the moment I see my beautiful Valkyrie and she takes my arm to walk down the aisle together. She's starting to show at eighteen weeks.

It's not our wedding.

I married her two weeks after I brought her back to my apartment, as soon as we could get the paperwork together to make it legal.

No, today is Chelle and Nikolai's wedding.

Chelle's brother, Zane, walks up the aisle behind us then Nikolai.

Chelle wanted a real wedding–an American wedding–so we are here, dressed to kill. Hopefully not literally today.

The men fan out behind the groom, our beautiful women arranged on the opposite side. I can't take my gaze off Kira, who is perfection in the strapless teal gown, tailored to make room for her expanding belly.

"Mama?" Benjamin stands uncertainly at the back.

The crowd laughs softly and murmurs in adoration.

Lucy and Ravil beckon to the boy, and he takes three

The Gatekeeper

slow steps, then races the rest of the way down the aisle and into Ravil's arms. Ravil picks him up and holds him as everyone stands for Chelle's grand entrance.

Nikolai tugs at his bowtie when he takes in the sight of her, clearly overcome.

It's a sweet and short ceremony with vows they wrote themselves, and then the party begins.

The band tunes up. Champagne is poured.

Chelle and Nikolai circulate in the crowd.

I take Kira's hand, and we find a spot against the rail to look at the water together.

"I love living on this lake," Kira murmurs.

"Do you?"

"Yes. It feels like Anya's always with me. The real Anya–the one from my childhood who made me laugh and took care of me."

"I'm glad." I kiss her temple. "Do you wish you had a wedding like that?"

Kira scoffs. "Me? Absolutely not. I mean, it was lovely, but I don't need any of that."

"No." I brush her hair back from her face. "You're a warrior, not a princess, aren't you?"

She smiles and shakes her head. "No more war. Just peace now."

It's true. While Kira has taken a position on my security team for the building, she spends her free time on more creative endeavors. Learning pottery from Kat. Baking. Taking kickboxing and yoga.

She's blooming into more and more happiness every day, expanding my own capacity for joy. Love. And yes, peace.

She's my best failure as gatekeeper, crashing past all my defenses, indelibly into my heart.

* * *

For **a special bonus scene with Kira and Maykl, join my newsletter.** If you're already a subscriber, the bonus content for all my books can be accessed using the button at the bottom of any newsletter.

Thank you for reading The Gatekeeper, the final book in the Chicago Bratva series. If you enjoyed it, **I would so appreciate your review**. They make a huge difference for indie authors like me.

If you're not already a member, I'd love to see you in **my Facebook Group, Renee's Romper Room.**

Want Another FREE Renee Rose book?

Read Her Royal Master for free here: https://hyzr.app.link/herroyalmaster

Want Another FREE Renee Rose book?

Other Titles by Renee Rose

Made Men Series

Don't Tease Me

Don't Tempt Me

Don't Make Me

Chicago Bratva

"Prelude" in Black Light: Roulette War

The Director

The Fixer

"Owned" in Black Light: Roulette Rematch

The Enforcer

The Soldier

The Hacker

The Bookie

The Cleaner

The Player

The Gatekeeper

Alpha Mountain

Hero

Rebel

Warrior

Vegas Underground Mafia Romance

King of Diamonds

Mafia Daddy

Jack of Spades

Ace of Hearts

Joker's Wild

His Queen of Clubs

Dead Man's Hand

Wild Card

Contemporary

Daddy Rules Series

Fire Daddy

Hollywood Daddy

Stepbrother Daddy

Master Me Series

Her Royal Master

Her Russian Master

Her Marine Master

Yes, Doctor

Double Doms Series

Theirs to Punish

Theirs to Protect

Holiday Feel-Good

Scoring with Santa

Saved

Other Contemporary

Black Light: Valentine Roulette

Black Light: Roulette Redux

Black Light: Celebrity Roulette

Black Light: Roulette War

Black Light: Roulette Rematch

Punishing Portia (written as Darling Adams)

The Professor's Girl

Safe in his Arms

Paranormal
Two Marks Series

Untamed

Tempted

Desired

Enticed

Wolf Ranch Series

Rough

Wild

Feral

Savage

Fierce

Ruthless

Wolf Ridge High Series

Alpha Bully

Alpha Knight

Bad Boy Alphas Series

Alpha's Temptation

Alpha's Danger

Alpha's Prize

Alpha's Challenge

Alpha's Obsession

Alpha's Desire

Alpha's War

Alpha's Mission

Alpha's Bane

Alpha's Secret

Alpha's Prey

Alpha's Sun

Shifter Ops

Alpha's Moon

Alpha's Vow

Alpha's Revenge

Alpha's Fire

Alpha's Rescue

Alpha's Command

Midnight Doms

Alpha's Blood

His Captive Mortal

All Souls Night

Alpha Doms Series

The Alpha's Hunger

The Alpha's Promise

The Alpha's Punishment

The Alpha's Protection (Dirty Daddies)

Other Paranormal

The Winter Storm: An Ever After Chronicle

Sci-Fi

Zandian Masters Series

His Human Slave

His Human Prisoner

Training His Human

His Human Rebel

His Human Vessel

His Mate and Master

Zandian Pet

Their Zandian Mate

His Human Possession

Zandian Brides

Night of the Zandians

Bought by the Zandians
Mastered by the Zandians
Zandian Lights
Kept by the Zandian
Claimed by the Zandian
Stolen by the Zandian

Other Sci-Fi

The Hand of Vengeance
Her Alien Masters

About Renee Rose

USA TODAY BESTSELLING AUTHOR RENEE ROSE loves a dominant, dirty-talking alpha hero! She's sold over two million copies of steamy romance with varying levels of kink. Her books have been featured in USA Today's *Happily Ever After* and *Popsugar*. Named Eroticon USA's Next Top Erotic Author in 2013, she has also won *Spunky and Sassy's* Favorite Sci-Fi and Anthology author, *The Romance Reviews* Best Historical Romance, and *has* hit the *USA Today* list over a dozen times with her Chicago Bratva, Bad Boy Alpha and Wolf Ranch series, as well as various anthologies.

Renee loves to connect with readers!
www.reneeroseromance.com
renee@reneeroseromance.com

- facebook.com/reneeroseromance
- twitter.com/reneeroseauthor
- instagram.com/reneeroseromance
- amazon.com/Renee-Rose/e/B008AS0FT0
- bookbub.com/authors/renee-rose
- tiktok.com/@authorreneerose

Printed in Great Britain
by Amazon